The Key

GARY T. BRIDEAU

THE KEY

Copyright © 2023 Gary T. Brideau.

All rights reserved. No part of this book may be used or reproduced by any means, graphic, electronic, or mechanical, including photocopying, recording, taping or by any information storage retrieval system without the written permission of the author except in the case of brief quotations embodied in critical articles and reviews.

iUniverse books may be ordered through booksellers or by contacting:

iUniverse
1663 Liberty Drive
Bloomington, IN 47403
www.iuniverse.com
844-349-9409

Because of the dynamic nature of the Internet, any web addresses or links contained in this book may have changed since publication and may no longer be valid. The views expressed in this work are solely those of the author and do not necessarily reflect the views of the publisher, and the publisher hereby disclaims any responsibility for them.

Any people depicted in stock imagery provided by Getty Images are models, and such images are being used for illustrative purposes only. Certain stock imagery © Getty Images.

ISBN: 978-1-6632-5530-3 (sc)
ISBN: 978-1-6632-5531-0 (e)

Library of Congress Control Number: 2023915018

Print information available on the last page.

iUniverse rev. date: 08/11/2023

Contents

Character Descriptions..vii

Storyline...ix

Chapter 1   Who am I...1

Chapter 2   Confrontation..8

Chapter 3   A failed plot..17

Chapter 4   Breakup...24

Chapter 5   The real Susie..31

Chapter 6   Patsy, among the missing..................................37

Chapter 7   Walking again 44

Chapter 8   Retaliation 51

Chapter 9   The past 57

Chapter 10   The one behind it all 64

Chapter 11   The truth revealed...71

Chapter 12   A tight squeeze 77

Chapter 13   Clearing the air..85

Chapter 14   Patsy Corrects Softy 92

Chapter 15   Doubleganger Returns 98

Epilogue...103

Short stories

Peach Nuclear Poer 107

The mystery by the beach 108

Chloe's Surprise Adventure...111

The Peril's of Water..120

Predictions 127
Why Did The Light Bulb Blow Out 133
The Future 135
The Unicorn 140
The Long Trip Home 142

Character Descriptions

Heather: is from Earth. She met her husband Mike when he was stranded there. She is five feet five eight tall in her mid-thirties with very curly red hair and freckles.

Mike: He is in his mid-thirties and a makeup artist for his acting group, Mike, and Company. *His home planet is* Haskell Prime, and he is married to Heather from Earth.

Holly: Mike and Heather adopted Holly, an albino sprite. She was born to King Mex and Isabella. Because Holly was an Albino, the King kicked her out of the palace. Holly was healed of albinism by the Blue Pixie Sap Phiri.

Patrick: a leprechaun or Patrick Seamus, Fionn Oisin Colm O'Donnagái O'Brien

He is thirty-eight inches tall, a leprechaun from Kylee.

Alexis Rosenthal O'Brien: is 29 years old and has bright red hair in a pixie. She has freckles on her face and is a petite four 'seven "tall. Alexis Where's Silver wire-rimmed glasses and likes listening to Mozart, married to Patrick O'Brian.

Susie J. Parkers: Very little is known about her, but she is in her forties and carries a gold key.

Chrissy: is a pixie thirty-six inches tall from the planet Slandor and is the doctor at the Institute.

Frank: a tall sleazy well-dressed man in his forties; with short black hair.

Dina: a tall woman dressed in a long forest green dress, green hair with flowers, and a gold crown. Who is an ancient computer program from the Odessa era?

Patsy J Mullens: A Mandroid, she is mid-thirties was born in the city of Odessa, on the planet Pharez, the garden of the galaxy about a thousand years ago. At the age of twenty-three, she had a horse-riding accident that left her completely personalized. Professor Tatsuya had compassion on the young woman and designed a new body for her that he called a Mandroid.

Softy Mullens: mechanical contrivance from the key and is an exact duplicate of Patsy.

Jeff Stearns: Is in his thirties and is five feet ten inches tall with medium-length hair. He was born in the city of Odessa 1000 years ago. Don't because of the brutal assault on him; her brain was put into the body of a Mandroid and has survived through the years.

Tom Marks: A Mandroid, he is in his mid-thirties was born in the city of Odessa, on the planet Pharez, the garden of the galaxy smart, cunning and has been on trouble with the law many time.

Alice Birdson: A Mandroid, She is in her mid-thirties and is quiet and shy. She was born in the city of Odessa, on the planet Pharez, the garden of the galaxy

Terrie Joan Ramsey: A Mandroid, with short black hair and was born in the city of Odessa, on the planet Pharez, the garden of the galaxy. Terrie is cunning

Storyline

A young woman wakes up on a park bench dressed in a long evening gown on a bright sunny afternoon. She can't remember her name, who she is, or how she got there. But in her purse is a gold scrolled key. While she is trying to find out her identity people are trying to kill her and steal the key because it Wheedled a strange power.

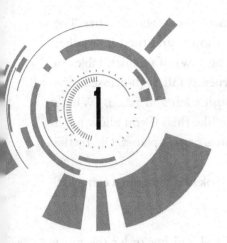

Who am I

On a warm summer evening, a woman in her mid-twenties with short brown hair dressed in a tight dark blue evening gown. She woke on a park bench, sat up, slowly scanned her surroundings, then questioned, "Where am I, and how did I get here?" The woman thought for a moment, then muttered, "I can't remember anything about my life," She searched in her black diamond scrolled purse for something which would tell her who she was and found a gold scrolled key some four inches long. The woman continued to search her bag and found a small brown leather pouch. Upon opening it, she took out a white driver's license with the name, Susie Joan. Parkers on it and enough money to buy dinner.

Susie studied the moon rising in the east, thinking, "I can feel much better on a full stomach, and walked to Kitty's Diner three blocks away. She ordered the Special in the diner, a large coffee, and a red berry pie for dessert. After a hearty meal, Susie went into the women's room and took off all her clothes to see if any of the tags on her clothing would give her a clue who she was, but there were no tags. After paying for her food, the gold key tumbled out of her purse and on the floor. The manager picked it up and stared at it for a good minute. Slowly handed it back to Susie and said, "The meal is free, and would you like something to take with you?"

"I sure would; what would you recommend,"

"The Blue Buffalo special and a tall glass of lemonade, and there is no charge,"

Susie made her way to the nearest shelter hoping to secure a bed for the night but couldn't shake the feeling someone was following her. The next morning Susie waited in line for her shower and then in another long line for her food. She stared at the long rows of wooden tables in the dining room, then sat at one in the corner. A tall, well-dressed man in his forties with short black hair sat on Susie's left and asked, "What's a classy dame like yourself doing in a place like this? If you allow me, I will have you sleeping in one of the best hotels on this planet. Oh, by the way, my name is Frank.

Susie glanced at Frank, then said, "You look like someone I can trust. What do you have in mind,"

"Come with me, and you will see,"

Frank brought Susie to a fancy diner and had her order the most expensive breakfast on the menu, then bought her new clothes.

At the end of the day, Susie relaxed on a dark blue plush sofa, enjoying a tall frosty glass of cold Iced tea in the luxurious King's suite at the Plaza Hotel.

Frank sat on her left and asked, "Susie, can you loosen your top? I want to massage your shoulders,"

A trusting Susie pulled her white blouse out of her slacks, undid the top four buttons, and allowed Frank to rub her shoulders. She softly moaned, "Ohhh, Frank; it feels so good, don't even think of stopping."

As Frank was rubbing Susie's shoulders, little by little, he slid his hands lower and lower on her chest.

Suddenly the words, you're in danger, flashed in her mind. Susie jumped to her feet, unaware Frank had opened her blouse, and shouted, "I don't like you grabbing my boobs. I'd rather wait in line for my shower than let you do that to me."

Knowing he was caught, Frank tried to smooth things over by saying, "I am sorry I got carried away; now, sit down so I can finish, and I won't do it again,"

"You can have your fancy garbage; I'm going back to the shelter,"

Just then, a midget barged into the room and said, "Come with me because you have an important call in the lobby.

As soon as Susie was in the hall, the midget said, "Patrick O'Brian here to rescue you. He then looked away and stated, "Lassie, please close your blouse,"

Susie shook her head, then staggered sideways, saying, "I feel weird,"

Patrick took Susie's hand, saying, "You'll be safe in me room, then you can tell me why you are mixed up with a Crum Bum like Frank,"

Susie woke up the next day at noon, stared at Patrick taking her pulse, and asked, "Am I sick? Or is it a reason to hold my hand,"

"First, tell me why you allowed Frank to get super friendly with you,"

Susie went to sit up but fell back on the bed, holding her head and saying, "My head is spinning. Can we talk later?" She sat on the edge of the bed three days later, stretched, saying, "That was a great nap, Patrick: what's on the menu for dinner,"

Patrick glanced at his watch, saying, "Lassie, you've been sleeping for over four days. I think Frank put a mickey in your iced tea, which tells me he was trying to dupe you into something,"

Frank treated me like a queen until he got fresh with me in the hotel room,"

Patrick asked, "Where did you meet Frank,"

"I was having breakfast in the shelter when he sat beside me. He seemed nice, so I trusted him until he played with my boobies,"

"And you were in the shelter because,"

"I woke the other day on a park bench in my evening gown, and I don't know who I am, where I am, or how I got here, and that was the first place I thought of,"

"Did Frank give you the drink?"

"Yes. Frank said the drink was made especially for me,"

Susie took the key out of her purse, showed it to Patrick, and asked, "Do you know what is so important about this,"

Patrick picked up Susie's pocketbook and asked, "Where did you get this? Because each diamond is at least one carrot. Patrick then studied the key and said, "I heard fantastic stories about a key like this, but I thought they were just fairy tales. One more question, if your mind is a total blank concerning your past and identity, how do you know your name?"

"I found a driver's license in a small bag with Susie J Parkers' name, and I assumed that's who I am."

Patrick waved a foot-long silver wand over the license, and the readout on the wand read, female, 35 years old, Susie J Parkers was born on the planet HP 5. Patrick waved the wand over Susie to check her DNA, but the readout on the medical wand said, no DNA found; please select the android setting and continue.

Patrick put the wand on Android, waved it in front of Susie, and was shocked at what he found.

Susie inquired, "Patrick, what's wrong?"

"You better sit down for this," stated Patrick as he accessed the printer supplied by the hotel and printed out the results and gave it to Susie.

Susie read, "The Android was born in the city of Odessa, on the planet Pharez, the garden of the galaxy, about a thousand years ago. At 23, she had a horse-riding accident that left her completely paralyzed. Professor Rollins had compassion for the young woman and designed a body for her called a Mandroid. He transplanted her brain into the skull of the Mandroid using a fluid to surround the brain to reduce aging. The spinal cord goes down the back eight inches and connects to a black box that turns the signals from the brain into light energy that travels through fiber-optic to the different parts of the body. All the organs in this body are artificial except the brain, which is human in origin, but she still can eat, sleep, and do all the normal functions of a woman except having children. The artificial heart pumps real blood, and the artificial lungs supply oxygen to the brain.

Susie stared at Patrick and asked, "Does that mean I am a robot? Strange, I don't feel like one,"

"It appears to be, but I should give you a physical to be sure."

Susie stared at Patrick, saying, "Nice try, Pervert, but I am not falling for that line of malarkey,"

After Patrick showed Susie his Credentials, she went into the bathroom, came out three minutes later wearing only a white bath towel, then sat on the bed.

During the physical, Patrick opened Susie's towel to check her stomach. She thought Patrick was going to assault her and shouted, "What do you think you are doing, Pervert," she then went to hit Patrick.

He blocked her attempt by pushing her right arm back and removed it from her shoulder. Susie went to hit Patrick with her other hand, and he took that arm off and pulled off both legs because she tried to kick him.

A terrified Susie lay on the bed thinking Patrick was going to kill her and began screaming for help.

Patrick showed Susie her arms and leg, saying, "I am not going to hurt you, settle down and I'll put them back on,"

A shocked Susie stared at her limbs with her mouth open and said with tears streaming down her face, "You cut my arms and legs off. Why,"

Patrick covered Susie with a blanket, sat on her right side, and said softly, "I am not going to hurt you, and I didn't mean to take off your limbs. It seems you are a Mandroid, meaning you are a human and an android, look at your limbs and see for yourself,"

"I think your scanner is malfunctioning, and give me back my limbs you Pervert,"

"Understood, but when I say Odessa, what comes to mind?"

The Garden of the Galaxy and the sunken gardens of Pharez where a smooth-talking Horace raped me and Professor Rollins,"

Patrick questioned as he put Susie's limbs back on, "Do you want to talk about Horace? It will help to heal the hurt,"

Susie sat up and stated, "It was the day before my accident. I was strolling through the Exotic Sunken Gardens late in the afternoon in my blue, short set and met Horace, the boy I knew in school. He found a secluded place in the garden where we could be alone. We talked, catching up on old times for hours. The fragrance of the flowers had a soothing effect on me as I lay on my back, looking up at the sky, and fell asleep. I woke and was horrified because he was in the middle of raping me, so I screamed, "Get off me!" Susie broke down and cried, "Why did he do that to me, why,"

Patrick stated, "Let me help you get dressed, then I'll pray to the Lord Jesus to heal you of the hurt and fear,"

As Susie was putting on her blouse, a petite four foot seven inches tall woman in her late twenties with bright red hair done up in a pixie and freckles on her face. Wearing silver, wire-rimmed glasses clad in dark green shorts and a white blouse, walked into the room, stared at Susie, and screamed, "Husband of mine! What are you doing with that woman? Or do I want to know,"

Patrick showed a weak smile and asked, "Did you bring the body scanner,"

"It's in the briefcase I'm carrying. Now before I kick your butt, tell me what you were doing with her," Alexis then let go a long, loud screech,

Patrick stated, "Susie, this is me, wife Alexis.

A nervous Susie swallowed hard, then said, "Your husband has been a perfect gentleman and has been helping me get my memory back,"

Alexis opened the briefcase, took out some resilient material bars and plastic sheeting, and built a 7-foot high and 2-foot square rectangle box. Alexis then asked, "Susie, do you have any metal on you,"

"Outside of an underwire booby catcher, no,"

"Please remove it then, step in the scanning cage,"

Some ten minutes later, Alexis uploaded the scanned file to Patrick's laptop computer and asked, "What 'Ch got,"

Patrick stated, "Susie is definitely a Mandroid; she has a human brain kept alive by the artificial organs pumping blood and oxygen to it. But it is hard to tell if this is Susie or another one of Professor Rollins's Mandroid that survived the test of time. But Susie did tell me about Horace molesting her in the garden, which happened to Patsy from the Pharez solar system,"

Alexis sat in front of the laptop and said, "Computer, show me the historical records of the Pharez solar system."

A female voice stated, "A thousand years ago, there were three planets in the Pharez solar system, Milichiids, Hortensias, and Pharez: with planet Milichiids being the closest to the sun and Pharez being the last planet in this system. There were over ten billion people living on the three worlds, not including the people who lived on the moon of Stadium where the garden of the galaxy was located,"

Alexis asked, "Computer, are there any records of Horace Stubs,"

The computer replied, "Horace Stubs, also known as, The Garden Romeo because of the large number of women he seduced there,"

Alexis then asked, "Computer, how many Mandroids did Professor Rollins build,"

The computer replied, "Professor Rollins was a well-known physicist and lived on the planet Milichiids in the Pharez solar system until it was destroyed in a cataclysmic explosion,"

Alexis asked, "Computer, tell me how many Mandroids Professor Rollins made,"

The computer answered, "Professor Rollins built five Mandroids.

One of Tom Marks, Jeff Stearns, Patsy Mullens, Alice Birdson, and Terrie Joan Ramsey. But there are no records to what happened to them."

Patrick stared at Susie and said, "You are either Patsy Mullens, Alice Birdson, or Terrie Joan Ramsey.

2

Confrontation

The following day Susie woke to someone pounding on her door. She staggered to it in her bright yellow PJs, saying, "Save the pieces; I'm coming."

Upon opening it, Frank pushed her aside and entered, saying, "I set you up in this luxurious hotel, and this is how you repay me."

"You were way out of line when you squeezed my boobies; now please leave," and turned to walk away.

Frank ripped off Susie's PJ top, spun her around, and slammed his hand on the right side of her chest, turning her off.

Susie's lifeless body fell to the floor with a loud thud and lay motionless until Frank took a long thin knife from his pocket to slice her open.

Susie turned herself on and kicked Frank in his stomach, saying, "Not today, Pervert."

An angry Frank lunged for Susie with his knife, slicing her side and causing her to stagger backward.

Patrick rushed into the room, shouting, "Leave the lassie alone!"

Frank turned, saying, "Or what, shorty,"

Patrick quickly rubbed his hands together, stretched them out in front of him, sending a charge of electricity dancing around Frank, then said, "That was just a warning; the next one will fry you to a crisp,"

Frank raised his hands and left, saying, "The next time, I'll succeed,"

Susie lay on the bed so Patrick could use the healing generator resembling an electric razor to close up the gash on her side, and she asked, "Why is this creep, Frank, after me,"

"I don't know, lassie, but Alexis and I will find out,"

After Susie sat up and was about and dressed, Alexis walked in and stated with her hands on her hips, "This is the second time I caught you in Susie's room when she's half naked,"

"I came in to check on Susie and found Frank attacking her; as you can see, he tore her top off and sliced her side."

Alexis picked up the torn PJ top and touched the blood on the carpet, saying, "I believe you, but what is so important about Susie's chest,"

Susie stated, "I just found out when someone hits me just above my left boob, I pass out,"

Alexis stood in front of Susie with her hand outstretched and asked, "May I,"

"Sure, go ahead,"

Alexis gently placed her hand on Susie's chest, felt a raised area, and pressed it.

Susie's arms dropped to her side as her limp body fell back on the bed; Alexis than said, "I guess you were right, Patrick, but why does Frank want to turn Susie off and cut her open? It doesn't make sense,"

Patrick stated, "Some years back, Patsy spoke to Carrie, a woman in her mid-fifties with salt and pepper hair who did an extensive study on the city of Odessa and all about Mandroids. Patsy then talked to Dina, an ancient solid, three-dimensional computer program from the Odessa era. About a year ago, Thor bought an abandoned warehouse on the planet, Dicapl, and had Carrie and Dina recreate a segment of the city of Odessa. I'll guarantee you; that Frank got his information from one of them or the re-creation of Odessa city unless someone hid something of value inside of Susie, and Frank has found out about it."

Patrick then pushed and rubbed every inch of Susie's body, searching for something hidden under the skin. Then a short time later, Patrick shook his head, saying, "You can get dressed, lassie; I can't find anything unless it's hidden deep inside."

Alexis stated, "I checked the scanned file you did on Susie yesterday, and she's clean. Was Frank trying to put something inside Susie to use her as a courier? First, he put her to sleep by giving her a sedative in her iced tea, then rubbed her chest as if he were looking for her off switch."

Susie stated, "There is one person who knows about my off switch beside me, and that is Teeny."

Patrick stated, "Teeny is not into espionage because if he were, Thor, The Galaxy Sentinel would have him locked up in a heartbeat,"

At the re-creation of Odessa City on the planet Dicapl, Susie stepped out of Patrick's car, scanned the beautiful garden, and froze as a collage of distorted memories flashed through her mind.

Alexis touched Susie's shoulder and asked, "Are you alright,"

"Give me a minute; all this brings back memories of what happened to me here,"

Dina, wearing a long forest green dress, green hair with flowers, and a gold crown, approached and said, "Welcome to Odessa, the Garden of the Galaxy. Feel free to stroll around the exotic garden of Pharez, or step back a thousand years and explore the city of Odessa," Dina stared at Susie and asked, "Patsy, is that you,"

"No, I'm Susie,"

"You must have had a traumatic experience that created a memory block, but why do you have a different face? Would you mind if I check out your system to see if everything is running right,"

Dina placed her hands on Susie's shoulders, turned into a white mist, and entered Susie as a thin stream.

Susie's eyes widened as her body stiffened until Dina left three minutes later and said, "Whoa, what a mess in there; it looks like someone worked you over pretty good. I reinflated your stomach and lower track. Fixed the connections to your aorta and realigned your facial structure. All you have to do is slap your jaw a few times to activate the repairs,"

Susie slapped her jaw three times with her hands, causing her system to repair itself.

Patrick stared at Susie as her face slowly changed to that of Patsy and asked, "Dina, what do you think took Susie's memory,"

"The way her insides were messed up, I'd say someone gave her a good pounding which traumatized her,"

Dina turned to Susie and asked, "What do you remember,"

"Waking up on the park bench in my evening gown. Horace Stubs who raped me when I fell asleep in the garden," Susie slowly walked to a fiery red bush with yellow flowers, picked a flower, put it to her nose, and said, "I was sitting under a bush just like this, an orange-colored tabby jumped in my lap, curled up, and purred. A medium-built man in a business suit sat next to me and handed me the gold-scrolled key I had in my purse. What I am doing with it today, I don't know, but I am not a thousand years old, and I am not Patsy, who lived back then. I just look like her,"

Susie showed Dina the key and said, "This is the key the man with the Tabby gave me,"

Dina took it and rubbed it with her hands, saying, "There is an old legend about a gold key that would unlock a vast treasure, but the key was lost thousands of years ago,"

Susie inquired, "Who told that sleaze ball, Frank, where my shutoff switch is,"

Dina stated, "He was here last week asking all kinds of questions, but no one told him how to shut you off,"

"By any chance, did you re-create Professor Rollins's laboratory where he created me,"

"Of course," stated Dina, "The city of Odessa would not be complete without a tour through Professor Rollins's lab with a reproduction of you,"

Inside the massive warehouse, Dina led Susie, Patrick, and Alexis, to Rollins's lab in the middle of the mockup city and said, "As you can see, his lab is complete right down to the last detail,"

Susie was shocked as she glared at her duplicate lying on a metal table without anything on and the blueprints of the inner workings next to it. Covered it with a white sheet saying, "Why don't you put it on a large screen with the caption; come and see a naked Susie,"

Carrie, dressed in tan slacks and a white blouse, approached Susie, and asked, "Is there a problem,"

Susie snapped back, "How dare you televise an indecent me lying on a table. Susie took the schematics of the body and gave them to Carrie, saying, "Because of this, Frank tried to shut me down and kill me twice,"

Carrie stated, "Patsy, the last report was you were missing and presumed dead, so we put a replica of you in Rollin's lab as a memorial, but if we knew you were still alive, we would not have done it. Is there anything I can do for you,"

"How many times do I have to say I am not Patsy, who lived a thousand years ago in Odessa? Now, put some clothes on that thing; you say she is me!" demanded Susie.

Just then, an elderly couple touring Odessa city walked into the lab. The old man quickly approached Susie and said, "Sweet, here's that Mandroid everyone's been talking about,"

His wife stared at Susie, saying, "People are making a lot of hullabaloo, about this? Her head is too small, her butt is too big, and her legs are way out of proportion,"

Susie remained motionless, listening to the cryptic remarks of the elderly woman, then stated, "My butt is not big, and Sir, if you touch my boobs one more time, I'm gonna slap you,"

The wife stated, "I think it's so cute the way you made that Mandroid seem alive,"

Susie snatched the coffee out of the man's hand, took a swallow, and said, "You have way too much sugar in your coffee, Sir, and yes, I am the real Susie,"

The wife stated, "There's no such thing as a Mandroid; it's all a fancy ploy to get people in here,"

Susie took hold of her right arm with her left hand, removed it, pointed it at the woman, saying, "You lady, are too critical about everything,"

The wife of the elderly man stared at Susie's detached arm, grabbed her husband's hand, and rushed out the door with him, with Susie snickering.

"Can your sick jokes, Dina, and I run a respectable establishment,"

"You call exposing my bare body to the public respectable? Just about everyone has seen me in the buff,"

Carrie stared at Patsy's likeness, then at Susie and stated, "It's you, it's really you; I thought you were dead,"

"I am not Patsy, I just look like her, but because she does, that sleaze ball Frank is trying to kill me thanks to you,"

Carrie thought for only a minute before saying, "Professor Rollins put a subatomic generator in you, ah Patsy, to run the heart, Frank could be after that, but I don't know why,"

Patrick put a closed sign on the lab door and said, "This exhibit is closed until further notice,"

"Why close the lab," questioned an aggravated Carrie.

Patrick stated, "I want to know what Frank is up to and for the safety of Susie."

As they strolled through the City of Odessa an hour later, Susie picked up a newspaper and screamed, "Dina, get your scrawny hide here this minute,"

Dina appeared two feet in front of Susie and asked, "You bellowed, O boisterous one,"

Susie showed her the photo of her replica in Rollins's lab with the headlines that read, what is the mystery behind this thousand-year-old robot? The story inside,"

"Do you see this picture of a replica of me without anything on, and has it listed as a robot? Thanks to you, everyone is going to think I'm Patsy,"

Dina smiled, saying, "It's not a real newspaper, Carrie and I thought it would be cute,"

Susie stated through clenched teeth, "I don't think it is cute; get rid of them, Now,"

Alexis tapped Susie's shoulder, saying, "There is something strange going on in your purse,"

Susie looked in her pocketbook, took out a glowing, vibrating gold scrolled key, held it in front of her face, and vanished.

Days later, Susie woke in the same fancy dress on a park bench on a cold, wet morning and sat up wondering who she was and how she got there."

Patrick tapped her side, saying, "Welcome back, lassie, Alexis, and I was wondering when you were going to return. Do you remember what happened or where you went,"

Susie put her head in her hands, saying, "Give me a minute to gather my thoughts,"

Susie's eyes suddenly widened as she stared at Patrick, fell to her knees, wrapped her arms around him, and cried, "All I can remember are dark images moving around as I walked down a path surrounded by trees,"

Susie went to stand but fell on her face writhing in pain for a good minute. She then sat up and asked, "Patrick, how can I be a Mandroid and have so much pain? Professor Rollins didn't program that into me, at least I don't think he did,"

Patrick stated, "He probably did, but because of a glitch in your system, it wasn't activated until you were beaten, which brought the system online,"

Susie went to stand and shrieked in pain, saying, "My back, my back!"

Patrick quickly glanced around to make sure no one was watching, unzipped the back of Susie's dress, and exclaimed, "Good Lord will you look at that!"

Alexis stood behind her husband and asked, "What's that thing doing on her back? Those things are excruciating once they attach themselves to you,"

Patrick took hold of the foot-long, eight-legged, black, and red bug by its neck, gently pulled it off, then killed it.

Susie flexed her shoulders, saying, "That feels a whole lot better. What did you say that nasty thing was,"

"Some kind of a bloodsucker, and it looks like one of the nastiest creatures ever lived. Come lassie, you need some rest, and I know just the place,"

At Patrick's summer log cabin home, Susie put on a skimpy green two-piece bathing suit, slipped into the churning waters of a Jacuzzi, and fell asleep.

She woke an hour later, being hauled out of the hot tub with a hand over her mouth; then, a hand slammed on her off button. Susie turned herself back on and struggled to free herself from the kidnapper to no avail and was thrown to the ground.

Too weak to struggle, Susie let her body go limp, then waited for the cold steel of a knife to penetrate her body and passed out.

Susie came too, hours later in the dark, lying on a cold cement floor dressed in her skimpy two-piece bathing suit. Felt her arms and body for lacerations and found none.

A light came on, revealing rock walls, and she knew she was in the basement of a home. Frank slowly walked down the stairs and up to Susie and said, "If you cooperate, I will give you some clothes to wear. He took the gold key out of her purse and asked, "What does this gold key do,"

"That's a key? It sure doesn't look like one,"

Frank backhanded her across the face saying, "Don't get smart with me; tell me what this key is for,"

Susie smiled, saying, "How about if we have some fun first," and took hold of the bottom half of her bathing suit.

When Frank looked down to unbuckle his belt, Susie grabbed him by the throat and squeezed until he passed out, put on his clothes, and raced upstairs. Spotted a foot-long sausage, and pepper grinder, and a bottle of Iced Tea on an Oak table, grabbed them, and ran outdoors."

On a full stomach, Susie slowly scanned the dense forest, saw footprints on the ground, and followed them. Some twenty-one minutes later, she heard someone moaning and stopped to figure out where it was coming from. She darted west for two hundred yards and found the young man's leg. Susie slowly walked east and found another arm and two legs.

Then a male voice shouted, "Hey, Meat Head, over here!"

Susie knelt on the right side of a male torso in his white BVDs and asked, "Having one of those days when nothing goes right? By the way, where are your clothes,"

"Can the chitchat lady and put my limbs back on, that's if you know how to do it, you stupid woman,"

Susie dropped the limbs and turned to walk away when the young man said, "I'm sorry. Please help me,"

"What's your name,"

"Jeff Stearns, and let me tell you how to reattach my limbs,"

"I know how to do it, so be quiet and drop the Mandroid talk. You are a human with artificial limbs Like me,"

A shocked Jeff stated, "I am a Mandroid and the only one in existence,"

"Okay, whatever you say, then I'm a Mandroid too,"

"You're pulling my leg,"

Susie giggled and held up his leg, saying, "Actually, I am, see,"

Jeff laughed then said, "Cute, I never thought of that,"

Susie stared at Jeff saying, "I am not getting fresh with you, but I have to handle your bottom to reattach your legs."

"Can you get fresh with me later," stated Jeff smiling.

Once Jeff's limbs were back on, Susie took off her left arm to show Jeff she had artificial limbs too. Stared at Jeff, saying, "Until we find some clothes for you, you're gonna walk behind me,"

Jeff bellowed, "Not on your life, lady; I know the way out of this forest; you don't,"

"Look, Mister Macho, the last thing I want to do is to stare at you in your underwear all the way home, so get behind me or get lost,"

"Not gonna happen, lady,"

Susie belted Jeff just above his left breast; his arms went limp and fell backward like a tree. She then waited for him to open his eyes, but he didn't. She sat on the ground, sat Jeff up, leaned him against her chest, and wrapped her arms around him. Jeff opened his eyes and asked, "What are you doing,"

"Don't say a word; you need a woman's loving arms around you to help you relax,"

Some twenty minutes later, Susie stood and stared at Jeff, saying, "I'm wearing a two-piece bathing suit under my clothes so you can have the jeans,"

Jeff put on the pants, then said, "Thanks, but it's going to be dark soon, so we'd better make camp here. You make the fire, and I'll scare up some food,"

Sometime later, Jeff roasted a rabbit over a roaring fire and thanked Susie for holding him the way she did.

Later, as the fire was slowly dying, Jeff curled up to it and tried to get some sleep.

Susie stared at Jeff and thought, "Should I keep him warm? Is he going to assault me in my sleep,"

3

A failed plot

Early the next day, Susie woke with Jeff snuggled against her back and his hand on her thigh. He kissed her forehead, saying, "Good morning, Princess. I hope you didn't mind me keeping you warm last night,"

"I appreciated you snuggling up to me, but I held your hands to keep you from getting fresh with me in my sleep. Now, what's for breakfast beside tree bark,"

"I found a stream close by and caught a Salmon. By the way, what's with the fancy Key,"

"I don't know; I woke one morning on a park bench with no memory and that Key in my purse. Now give me a chunk of that fish before I starve to death,"

Susie took a bite of her fire-roasted fish and asked, "Since you are the travel expert, where are we, and how do we get out of this forest,"

"We are in Ashland, Oregon, on the north American continent. Frank has a personal portal to his cabin. That's how I got here,"

"And you know this because,"

"Because Frank kidnapped me and brought me here looking for something. When I didn't have it, he dismantled me and left me for dead. You came along two days later and rescued me,"

Susie stated, "Which means it may be months before we get back home, and that means we are stuck with each other until then,"

Susie sat on an old log and said, "Sit and tell me what you were like before you were put in your so-called Mandroid,"

Jeff stated, "I had turned thirty and landed a great job working as a security in the Sunken Garden. On the first day on the job, my boss informed me to be on the lookout for Horace Stubs, the Garden Romeo. He then told me about a young woman who had a serious horse-riding accident after being accosted by Horace. I immediately made up my mind to make that creep pay for what he did to her. About a week later, I caught him forcing himself on a young woman. But he hit me on the back of my neck, paralyzing me. However, my boss was nearby and drove his spear through his heart. I was awarded the medal of Valor and this new body. I only have one regret; I didn't get the chance to tell that woman I got the Garden Romeo. After I was released from the medical center, I spent the next five years looking for her," Jeff looked at Susie and said, "Now you tell me your story,"

Susie stated, "My story is short and sweet. I woke on a park bench with no memory. Now a midget named Patrick is trying to convince me I am a Mandroid from the city of Odessa. But I do remember having a horse-riding accident after being sexually assaulted by some jerk in the garden,"

"Seriously? You're the one I've been searching for all these years," stated a shocked Jeff.

"Back to the subject at hand. Where are we going to get the money to buy some clothes,"

Give me your shirt and shoes, and I'll go to Ashland and see what I can do,"

"Sound like a plan, but don't take too long because I'm gonna be hanging around these woods in a skimpy bathing suit,"

Outside Nobles Coffee Roasting in Ashland, Oregon, Jeff found some discarded pastel chock and some drawing paper. Made a sign, 'Portraits Done Here,' then drew a portrait of Susie. Some three hours later, Jeff earned over eight hundred dollars and made his way to the Greenleaf Restaurant, where he ordered two of their delicious hamburger specials, then bought some clothes for Susie.

Back in the woods, Jeff handed Susie her food, pink slacks, a white blouse, and shoes, saying, "We need to find our way south to Tammy-Lee's home in California."

"Who is she, one of your old girlfriends," snapped Susie.

She's an undercover agent who will put us in contact with Calistus and his wife, Su. They will help us get home,"

Before Susie had a chance to put on her new clothes, Frank stepped out from behind a tree, pointed an energy pistol at them, saying, "Very touching, Susie, but you are coming with me, and if your friend follows us, I'll kill him, and if you resist, I'll kill you too, now let's go."

Susie whispered in Jeff's ear, "Trust me," then hit Jeff above his left breast, causing him to go unconscious. Susie then muttered to herself, "I hate what I am about to do, and I pray the Lord will forgive me," and prayed what she was about to let Frank would keep him from killing her and Jeff. She lay on her back on the ground and said, "I am yours, Frank, for whatever you want to do,"

As Frank looked down to unbuckle his pants, Susie found a large rock and threw it at him striking him on the head, knocking him out.

A short time later, Frank slowly stood holding his head, saying, "What's the big idea hitting me with that rock?"

Susie pointed Frank's energy pistol at him saying, "I'll give you one minute to get out of my sight, or I'll shoot you where you stand,"

Frank took off running through the forest as Susie wildly fired at him.

Later, Susie sat on a fallen tree some distance away, put her head in her hands, and cried, "Lord, please forgive me for not trusting in you concerning Frank. But right now, I feel like Crap because I was going to let Frank do it to me to save my hide."

Jeff gently placed his hands on Susie's shoulders, saying, "You did what you had to do. Before you put your clothes back on how about if I give you a good back rub to help you relax,"

Susie lay on her stomach saying, "I am glad you are awake. Just a little lower on my back and to the left, yeah, that's the spot,"

While Jeff was massaging Susie's shoulders, he tried to force himself on her. She pushed him off, stood, and said, "Are you sure you're not the Garden Romeo because that's what he did when he forced himself on me,"

"I'm sorry I got a little carried away,"

"A little carried away," shouted Susie, "If I didn't stop you when I did, you would have raped me because it would have been against my will. Now stop staring at my boobies and give me my clothes,"

Jeff stated, "We need to be married ASAP,"

Susie began to be dizzy and had difficulty thinking straight and agreed to marry Jeff then lay with him all that day.

In Ashland the next day, Jeff brought Susie to the justice of the piece and married her. He then dragged her back into the forest and found a secluded spot.

A groggy Susie stared at Jeff unbuttoning his shirt and asked, "What are you doing,"

"We are married, so shut up and get ready to consummate our marriage,"

"Here and now?" asked a nervous Susie, "What if someone sees us,"

"Don't worry; no one will come by, so get ready to have some fun,"

Susie stared at Jeff and thought she had no other recourse but to do what he said.

An hour later, Jeff stood, brushed the dirt off of Susie, and asked, "What's wrong,"

Susie moaned, "A motel in Ashland would have been much better. But no, you had me lie on the cold ground with a twig sticking in my back while you went at it like a house afire. Now, if you will excuse me, I'm going to get dressed before someone walks by and sees me,"

"Not yet" stated Jeff, "I want to build a fire then snuggle with you in front of it,"

"Let me dress first," stated a determined Susie.

"No, that will spoil the fun," stated Jeff as he yanked Susie's clothes out of her hands.

The next morning, Susie dressed before Jeff could say anything, then said, "Now that's a wedding nightmare is over. Do you have any of the money left? Because I am starving,"

In Ashland, the couple stopped in the Morning Glory Café on Siskiyou Blvd for breakfast. Susie took a swallow of her coffee, glanced at Frank next to her and he stated firmly, "You are coming with me into the Men's room, and if your friend does anything to stop me, the both of you are dead,"

In the Men's room, Frank locked the door and then stated, "No more fulling around; my boss has grown tired of all the garbage you've been pulling. He wants what's inside you and the key, and he doesn't care how I get them."

Frank took an energy pistol from inside his shirt, pointed it at Susie, and fired.

A yellow Aurora formed around Susie, enveloped Frank, and vaporized him.

Susie's stood motionless in unbelief for two minutes, took a brilliant gold Scroll key out of her purse, held it up in front of her, and asked, "What is this thing? It transports me to wherever, and it just put a protective energy field around me when Frank tried to shoot me,"

Susie unlocked the men's room door as a tall man barged in and pushed her into one of the stalls to rob her,"

In the stall, Susie smiled, then stated, "I know what you need," She put her arms around his neck, then kneed him between his pocket, sending him on the floor groaning in pain. But before Susie could exit the men's room. The man grabbed her right shoulder, spun her around, and landed a hard right cross to her jaw, sending her sprawling on the floor.

Jeff walked into the men's room, saw Susie on the floor, stepped over her, and said, "I see you like to hit women; try me,"

Jeff caught the man's hand when he took a swing at him, twisted it, then landed a haymaker to his face, helped Susie up, and left.

Sometime later in Ashland Creek Park, Jeff placed a cold compress on Susie's jaw. Then asked, "What is it with you and violence, and what happened to Frank? He took you in the men's room to rough you up, and when I walked in, some other guy was there,"

"You are not going to believe this. Frank shot me but an energy field of some kind formed around me and then vaporized Frank. I took the Key out of my purse, and it was glowing,"

"You're right; I don't believe it,"

The next day Susie and Jeff huddled under a picnic shelter watching the deluge of rain in a rest area just off Interstate 5 south in Hornibrook, California. When it stopped, Susie heard a familiar voice behind them say, "Well don't you look like a drowned rat,"

Susie spun around and squealed, "Patrick! Where did you come from, and where is Alexis,"

"She's in the woman's room, but what I want to know is how did you get here,"

"Patrick, this is Jeff Stearns; Frank dragged me out of the pool, drugged me, and brought me to his cabin. I escaped and found Jeff's arms and legs scattered over the forest; put him back together, and the two of us have been trying to make it to Tammy-Lee's home in California. Oh, Jeff and I are married,"

Patrick turned to Jeff and said, "There is a hotdog vendor in the south part of this rest area; indulge yourself,"

After Jeff happily went on his way for a hot dog, Patrick stared at Susie with a stern expression on his face and stated, "Are you sure you made the right decision concerning Jeff,"

"We were gonna be together for months, so Jeff thought it was the logical idea for us to marry,"

"Are you sure he's not working for Frank,"

"How can a sweet, kind, and gentle man like Jeff work for a cold, heartless man as Frank was,"

"What do you mean, was," asked Patrick.

"Frank took me into the men's room to kill me, but some type of energy formed around me and vaporized Frank. Then I told Jeff that there's something more to this Key than we realized. But I believe what Jeff said, the Key is something that can do weird things, and nothing more,"

Patrick took the Key out of Susie's purse, examined it then said, "I was able to pinpoint your location on the scanner because this Key is giving off a unique Energy signal that can be picked up clear across the country. So don't let Jeff tell you otherwise,"

"But Jeff knows what he is talking about concerning the Key, so when we get back, I am giving it to him because it is a useless piece of junk. Oh, one other thing, Jeff and I will be living here because people here don't think we are weird. Oh, Jeff has a male friend looking for a good time, and he wants me to sleep with him for three nights, which I think will be fun,"

A shocked Patrick couldn't believe the garbage coming from Susie's mouth. He took his medical scanner out of his green bag, scanned Susie, and found traces of a toxin on her back. He watched Jeff approaching, finishing his third hot dog, and thought, *That guy does not act like a Mandroid,*"

Susie suddenly shouted, "Jeff!" she ran to him, jumped, landing with her legs straddling his body, threw her arms around his neck, and wouldn't stop kissing him.

Alexis pried Susie off Jeff, then escorted her for a hot dog. Patrick walked up to Jeff and stopped him by saying, "I don't know who you are working for, but you're not a Mandroid,"

"I don't care what you think I am. Susie put me together, and she thinks I am, so I am,"

"Your limbs may be robotic, but your torso is one hundred percent human,"

Jeff smiled, saying, "As the Planetary Alliance goes, they say I am a Mandroid which means I am protected by the Alliance. Susie can't testify against me because she's my wife, and in the Alliance, a wife can't testify against her husband. Soon as I get the Key, Susie and I will depart for parts unknown. When I gave Susie a back rub, I put a drug in her system that affected her mind, so anything I say, I'm right, and everybody else is wrong,"

Patrick stated, "You poor deluded idiot. On Earth, you have to have a blood test, which you didn't because if you did, it would have shown you were an alien, and Susie would have been classified as nonhuman, so you are not married to Susie,"

Patrick pointed to a Greyhound bus ready to leave, saying, "Your plot to get the Key has failed, be on it when it leaves or be dead,"

4

Breakup

Patrick rented a camper and camped in R-Ranch Klamath Campground until Susie's head was clear. Alexis gave Patrick a mug of coffee and asked, "How are we going to tell Susie that she is Patsy and is a Mandroid, and her home is on the other side of the galaxy,"

"We are going to have to wait for the right moment because she is emotionally linked to Jeff right now,"

The next day, Susie, dressed in jeans and a pink t-shirt, poured herself a mug of coffee, then sat on the riverbank staring at the rapids wondering why she used sex to keep Frank from killing her.

A thin woman in her mid-sixties clad in jean slacks and a blue tank top sat on Susie's left and asked, "Thinking about jumping in?"

"No, I'm just bugged at myself for what I did as a Christian. I mean, I knew better, yet I went and did it out of fear,"

"You can call me Dee, and you wanna tell me what's bugging you,"

"The other day, my husband and I were making our way south and camped in the woods just north of Ashland. The guy following us walked into the camp and threatened to kill my hubby and me if I didn't go with him. Like a fool, I lay on the ground, and offered my body to him. I've been a Christian for years, and I went and did a stupid stunt like that,"

Dee asked, "Did the man take you up on your offer,"

"Almost but I smacked him with a rock and knocked him out before he could do anything,"

Dee stated, "All Christians blow it every now and then. We are saved by the finished work of the Cross of Christ and not by our actions. So, we ask Christ forgiveness and go on vowing not to do it again. But I understand the way you feel. When I was serving the Lord in my thirties. I was married and had a great job. One day this guy where I worked started talking to me. I thought he was handsome and met him during my break and lunch. A starry-eyed me thought he was the best thing since sliced bread, and I wanted to see more of him. So, we met at the local diner in the evenings. One night after we left the diner, I sat in his car, and he gave me a kiss which led to another. My heart pounded like a trip hammer with each passionate kiss, and I didn't care where his hands were. After we made out, I went to his home for a cup of coffee and woke up the next morning in bed with him. Then for the next two weeks, I walked around feeling like crap condemning myself for letting him con me into going all the way with him. After reading the Word of God one day, the Lord helped me to understand forgiveness. I not only have to ask the Lord to forgive him, but I had to forgive myself as well,"

Susie stated," You're right, there is pleasure in sin for a season, but the end results are always bitter,"

After Dee left, Jeff sat on Susie's right and said, "We need to get out of here before someone catches us,"

Susie threw her arms around Jeff and asked, "I missed you; where did you go?"

Patrick thinks I'm working for Frank's boss and trying to steal the key from you, but I'm not. What do you say we go to the Bate & Bates Café for a cup of java so we can talk?"

Susie bowed her head, saying, "I don't think I should leave without telling Patrick where I am going and who I am with,"

Patrick is only going to put a damper on our relationship, and I don't think you want that. Do you,"

"Patrick and Alexis are helping me get my memory back, so I have to stay with them. But Patrick is right; how can we be married when we didn't have a blood test, and where is the marriage license? I think all you wanted was sex, so you used some loser to play the justice of the peace. One more thing, when it comes to being intimate with a woman, you suck bigtime,"

Jeff asked, "How can you say that when we've been through so much together,"

"I am saying it because my head is finally out of a fug that it was in ever since you rubbed my back. Now, if you will excuse me, I have to use the lady's room,"

"If I put something on your back to scramble your brains. Where did I get it from? It wasn't in the pants or shirt pocket because you wore them before you gave them to me,"

"Frank gave you the tube of cream when he caught up with us in Ashland."

"Why are you siding with Patrick all of a sudden when he's out to split us up?"

Susie glanced around, wondering, *"Why do I feel like someone is watching me,"* She said, "For all I know, Frank put you in the forest so I could find you, then put a tracking device on you. How else was he able to find us after we had a four-hour head start,"

"He's an excellent tracker,"

"Yeah, right, tell me another lie, why don't you? The tracking device is hidden inside one of your molars. That's how Frank was able to find us,"

Jeff grabbed Susie's right arm, saying, "You, wife of mine, are coming with me; like it or not," and began to drag her off.

"Let go of my arm," screamed Susie trying to break free.

Suddenly, Susie vanished, leaving Jeff wondering what had happened to her. He answered his cell phone, saying, "No, Sir, I didn't because she just up and disappeared,"

The voice on the other end said, "I don't care how you do it I want that gold key and what is inside her, or it will be your head. Is that clear,"

Susie woke sitting against a huge maple tree in the park dressed in jeans and a pale flowered t-shirt holding her left arm. She gazed at the red rash on her forearm, went to the Emergency room to have it checked out, and wound up in a hospital ward with six other women. A nurse showed her to her bed and said, "The doctor will see you in the morning."

"All I want is to have my left arm looked at, not to be locked up," but the nurse paid no attention to her as she walked away.

A short woman with short black hair, in her mid-thirties, clad in a dark gray robe and slippers, approached her, and whispered, "I don't know want planet you are from, but the skin on your left elbow is hanging and isn't bleeding. Let me fix you up then I'll tell you something that will make your head spin. Keep that gold key out of sight if you want to keep it; I'm Karen, and you?"

"Susie,"

With Susie's elbow patched up, Karen brought her into the Day Room and stated, "I'm from the planet HP-5 of the Planetary Alliance on the other side of the galaxy. I thought I get away from it all and take my vacation on Earth. To make a long story short, some Dip Wad shot me and was rushed to the hospital and wound up here. What about you?"

"My brains are scrambled and don't know how I got here or who I really am,"

Hay, wait a minute, You're Patsy from the city of Odessa. I've seen the reproduction of you in the Professor's lab,"

"A lot of people have been telling me that, but I just look like her, that's all,"

Karen quickly glanced around, then asked, "You want to get out of here? I have a plan, but it takes two people to pull it off,"

Susie thought, "She may be a few flowers short of a garden, but I'm going to go for it. She then said, "I'm in. what's your plan,"

Every evening at six, they pick up the dirty laundry; the man flirts with the head nurse for a good ten minutes, giving us time to hide in the laundry cart. When we are in the laundry room, one of us distracts him while the other knocks him out. Then it's a hop, skip, and a jump to where I hid my runabout, and we're home free,"

"And if we are caught,"

"It's foolproof,"

In the laundry room at six-thirty in the evening, Karen whispered to Susie, "You distract him, and I'll club him,"

Susie slowly stood, climbed out of the cart, smiled at the janitor, and said, "I have a nasty bruise on my chest; could you look at it? Please, but you'll have to unbutton my top because I have a bum hand,"

The janitor smiled with delight as he eagerly unbuttoned Susie's top. But before he got to the last button, Karen knocked him out.

Once the janitor was tied and gagged, the two women darted out the door.

Around fifteen minutes later, Karen climbed over a stone wall and raced across a field of tall grass and into a barn, ready to collapse.

Susie entered the rickety old barn and saw Karen pulling the tarp off a long silver sleek spacecraft. She paused for a moment, then asked, "Where in the world did you get that thing from,"

"Get in; we don't have much time,"

A hesitant Susie stated, "I ah don't think I wanna trust that thing of yours,"

"Suit yourself. Is there anyone you want me to contact,"

"Yeah, Patrick and Alexis,"

"Do you mean the leprechaun that can shoot lightning from his fingertips,"

"Yes, him,"

Karen gave Susie a goodbye hug saying, "Thank you for helping me escape that dark, dank dungeon; I owe my life to you. If you are ever on my side of the galaxy, drop in HP 5, and we'll paint the planet red. Now, stand back and watch out because my ship has a nasty backwash,"

Susie was halfway across the field when she heard a loud bang, turned around, and saw the barn explode and Karen's spaceship dart out. She hovered the ship above Susie's head, opened the side hatch, and hollered, "I'll never forget you; bye for now," and was out of sight in seconds.

A tall woman in her mid-forties with dark brown hair ran up to Susie, out of breath, and asked, "Did you see the alien in that spaceship that just took off?"

"I saw the UFO but no alien. Why,"

The woman stared at Susie, made a call on her cell phone, and said, "She's in the field with me. I'll do my best to keep her here," The woman turned to Susie and asked, "What possessed you to walk in the farmer's hay field,"

"My curiosity got the best of me, and I just had to check out that old barn. Then Bang, and it was gone, and a UFO shot out of it."

"I'm Joan. Hey, I have a thermos full of coffee in my car and some Donuts. You wanna sit underneath that big oak tree and get out of this hot sun for a bit,"

"That sounds like a great idea since I haven't had dinner yet,"

Sitting underneath the oak tree, Susie took a bite of her Boston Creme donut and asked, "Was that the first UFO you've seen,"

"No, it wasn't. About three years ago, I just got out of my car to walk into my house at about eleven thirty at night. I looked up and saw a huge triangle slowly and silently gliding across the night sky. What was weird, it never made a sound, and you,"

Susie hung her head, saying, "I don't know; I may have. I have memory loss and can't remember who I am or where I am from. I know my name is Susie Joan Parkers, and I found that out from a license in my purse."

A wide-eyed Joan stated, "We gotta get out of here,"

"Why,"

"I'll explain later; get in my car, so I can take you to my place and hide,"

An hour later, in Joan's ultramodern California-style ranch house on two acres of woodland. She put on a fresh pot of coffee and then said, "My full name is Susie Joan Parkers, and I lost my diamond studded purse with a 9-inch gold scroll key in it some months ago, and I've been sick about it ever since,"

Susie took her purse out of a cloth bag she had and asked, "Is this the perse you lost,"

"Yes, yes! This is it!" you see, I like to dig in old ruins and found this gold scroll key along with a woman manakin. I took it home, cleaned her up, and put my blue evening gown on her just for fun. But much to my surprise, she opened her eyes and had difficulty remembering her name or who she was,"

Susie took hold of her left arm and removed it, saying, "I think I am that woman. But I don't remember you or being in this house,"

Joan left the room and came back three minutes later with a white shoe box and said, "I left you in my home and went back to the dig sight the next day and found these things. But when I returned home, you were gone,"

Susie picked out of the box a blue translucent credit card with Patsy Mullens, age 23, Odessa City. Tears ran down Susie's cheeks as she picked up a photo of a blue stuffed bear that had black eyes and nose but no mouth and said, "Gideon, my little buddy," She picked up a light brown purse that had make up from a beauty shop on HP5. Something that looked like a cell phone, but she didn't know how to turn it on. Susie took out of the purse a small box of Kleenex, three gold coins, and a photo of her, standing next to Patrick and Alexis under a gold banner that read Happy Birthday Patsy. She stared at a hand full of small rocks with names and dates on them. Looked at Joan, said, "I," and collapsed on the floor, out cold.

5

The real Susie

Susie woke several minutes later on the couch, with Joan applying a cold cloth on her head, and Susie shouted, "We gotta find him!"

"Find who?" inquired Joan.

"My little buddy, Gideon,"

"It's gonna have to wait till tomorrow morning because it's too late to look for him now,"

Early the next day, at the ruins of an ancient city, Susie frantically began to dig in the dirt. Joan tapped her shoulder, saying, "I found you over here by this falling monolith. What I want you to do is try to remember where your little buddy was standing,"

With a sad countenance, Susie stated, "All I can remember is Gideon standing in front of me trying to ward off the attackers,"

Late that evening, Joan uncovered the dark blue paw of a stuffed bear underneath a large boulder and shouted, "Susie, I found your little buddy!"

Back at Joan's place, Susie cleaned up Gideon but couldn't figure out why he wasn't moving. Gave the bear to Joan, saying, "He's not a real live bear, but he does walk. Can you fix him?"

Joan thought that Patsy had a few flowers short in her garden. Placed Gideon on the kitchen counter and accidentally touched one of the brass buttons on his light blue vest, causing it to flip open. A surprised Joan studied the tiny computer circuit board inside the button, blew out the dirt with an aerosol can, then closed it.

Gideon stood on his feet, bowed to Joan, and scanned the room. When he saw Sally, he hopped off the counter and raced into her waiting arms.

With tears running down her face, Sally said, "Thank you so much for fixing him,"

Joan said, "Susie, I've never seen anything like him. Gideon shook his head no and motioned for some paper and a pen.

Gideon sat on Susie's lap and wrote, "Her name is not Susie, but Patsy J Mullens of the city of Odessa and is a Mandroid with something of great value inside her.

A stunned Joan stared at the note for a good minute before she asked, "Can I see the note,"

When Joan read the note, she gazed at Susie and said, "It is indeed a great pleasure to have someone from the lost city of Odessa in my home,"

Gideon then wrote, "Patsy, when was the last time you had a light mineral oil bath to soften your skin, and have you seen my katanas,"

"I can't remember the last time I had one, and I'll have to buy you some new swords,"

Joan raced out of the room, coming back three minutes later, and handed Gideon his blades. He bowed and placed them in their sheath on his back.

Late that afternoon, Patsy stared at a hot tub full of light mineral oil in Joan's basement and said, "You did this for me?"

"I figure I could use a soak in that stuff too; now, let's hop in sans bathing suits,"

Just as the two women were in the hot tub, Joan heard the front door open and moaned, "It never fails. As soon as I get in the shower or the hot tub, someone comes to the door,"

Before either of the women could make a move, a tall clean-shaven man dressed in black and brandishing a 44 Magnum approached the hot tub. They quickly grabbed their nearby towel to cover themselves, and Joan shouted, "Get out of my house right this minute!"

"Or what?" asked the man, "You're gonna throw me out the way you are. I don't think so," He walked to Joan, put his gun to her head, and asked, "Any last words before I kill you and your friend?"

"I'll go with you just don't hurt my friend," Stated Patsy.

"The boss told me to leave no witnesses, so she gets it first,"

The man glanced down when he felt someone tapping his right leg. Saw Gideon and went to kick him. He flipped sideways and sliced the man's right leg with his sword. The man quickly grabbed the bear to shove it under the oil. But before he could, Joan shoved her oil-soaked towel in the man's face, sprang out of the hot tub, tackled him, and pushed him on the floor, hammering his face with her fist.

Patsy hauled Joan off the attacker, saying, "Calm down, you got him. Let's get dressed and call the police. Gideon, make sure he doesn't go anywhere,"

After the attacker was hauled away by the police, Patsy sat at the kitchen counter with Joan and asked, "You wanna tell me why you went nuts on the guy?"

"It's a long story,"

"We have plenty of time,"

"It was a couple of years ago. I was relaxing on my back porch in my pink bathing suit, trying to get a tan. When I heard the front door open and a noise in the living room but paid no attention to it. The next thing I remember is coming too in the hospital with my head, arms, and body bandaged up and half of my furniture gone. That's when I vowed that next time some goon breaks into my home, I was going to kick his butt, so I did,"

Patsy made a pot of Cinnamon Spice Tea and brought it to the white gazebo surrounded by red roses in Joan's backyard. She placed the Ceramic teapot shaped like a rose on a round table we're Styrofoam cups. Poured Joan a cup of tea, then herself one, and said, "One more time. What is churning inside of you that you refuse to let go of? But this time, don't give me a sob story; I want the truth,"

Joan took a sip of her tea, then said, "I've known Bruce for over twenty years, and he was a great friend," or so I thought. About ten years ago, I was married and hired him to do the gardening for one hundred dollars a week. He showed up promptly every Saturday at seven AM, walked into my home without knocking, and made a pot of coffee. I would walk into the kitchen in my white robe with roses on it and sit at the counter drinking my coffee while he would regale me about his two children and ex-wife, not paying attention to my husband. I fell in love with him and flaunted myself so he would notice me, which he did. Hubby took off with another woman, and I took sick; Bruce was more than willing to give me a sponge bath once a week and to minister to my needs which I greatly appreciated. But one day, he walked into my home unannounced and told me how I was to be dressed when he was in my home. I was in my robe and stared at a man who was cold and formal. He then told me about the birthday party he had for his oldest daughter, who had turned ten. I almost cried as I thought, *"Why didn't you invite me? I met you for coffee four times a week after my husband left, helped me around the house, and you did the gardening. Then you pull a stunt like this,"* I passed it off as an attitude and continued to flirt with him, praying he would pay attention to me. But it became an emotional ride; he'd be sweet and kind for two or three days, then he turned into a drill sergeant. One day we went to a diner for lunch, he had his usual stack of pancakes, and I had a double cheeseburger with fries. We connected for the first time since I hired him, and I had a man in my life again. But when Bruce came to do the gardening a few days later, he was cold, formal, and distant. I tried to pass his attitude off and promptly sprained my ankle. Bruce smiled and went outside to do his gardening. After, we went out for coffee, and I listened as he went on about how his family was treating him. A short time later, Bruce walked to the door and watched me as I struggled to stand on my bad ankle. I looked at him and whispered, "Please help me," but he stood by the door like a statue watching me trying to walk on my bad foot. That's when I vowed not to let him hurt me again,"

"So, you've been holding all that hurt and hatred for Bruce ever since," stated Patsy.

"Pretty much,"

"Let it go and allow Christ to heal you through the finished work on the Cross,"

"Could you pray with me?"

Right after Patsy assisted Joan in prayer, Patrick and Alexis approached the pavilion, and Patrick asked, "Would you mind if we join you?"

Patrick poured his wife a cup of tea, then sat next to her, saying, "Susie, you are one difficult person to track. What brings you here,"

"The name is Patsy Mullins, and it'll be in my report how I got here," she stared at Patrick, pondering her following statement, then asked, "Have you heard of something called a Mandroid,"

Gideon waddled in, crawled up on Patsy's lap, then waved to Patrick.

Alexis stated, "A Mandroid is part Android and part human, but that's something we'll discuss later,"

Joan piped up and said, "I'm an archeologist, and I was digging around the old runes north of here when I found a woman's body and a gold scrolled key. I figured it was a manikin and a child's toy key. I took them home, cleaned them up, put my deep blue evening dress on the manikin, and gave her my expensive black diamond studded purse just for G, and C. Patsy is that manakin I brought home who disappeared along with the key and my expensive purse. Now, tell me what is going on,"

Patrick stated, "Answer me this. Patsy disappears with your expensive dress, purse, and a gold key. But you didn't report it to the police or call them when you found her but treated her as a friend. How do I know this? When my wife and I walked up, you were having tea with Patsy as if she was your best friend. As a matter of fact, you were looking to her for advice. If it were me, I would have had Patsy locked up in a heartbeat,"

"She gave me back my stuff, so I forgave her,"

"Are you planning to turn Patsy in for the reward offered for her capture?"

"I wouldn't think of doing such a dastardly thing to my friend Patsy,"

"Are you the famous Susie J. Parkers archeologist, the one who filed a claim saying Hank stole an ancient artifact from you so you could sell it for $1.2 million when Hank was the one who found it,"

Alexis stated, "Joan, you are known to make friends with people to get something from them, and when you have it, you drop them like a hot potato. Oh, and that diamond studded purse is not yours. It was your friend Jessica's. You told her the diamonds on the purse were worthless pieces of glass, and the appraiser lied to her about their worth. Jessica gave you the purse, thinking it was just a piece of trash when in actuality it's worth millions,"

Joan took a thirty-eight revolver that was tucked in the back of her slacks, pointed it at Patsy, saying, "You're coming with me because I'm going to cash you in for the $500,000, and don't even think about touching your hands to give me a shock Patrick, because did gazabo is grounded which means those fancy hands of yours won't work,"

Patsy stretched her hands towards Joan, saying, "The key I have on me word protect me, so put that gun away and don't do something stupid."

"I get the money whether you are dead or alive, so get a move on,"

When Patsy didn't move, Joan fired at Patsy to kill her. But an energy field instantly formed around Patsy, protecting her. The energy field then turned a bright red, enveloped Joan, causing her to scream in pain."

When the energy field had dissipated, Patsy checked Jones artery, saying "She's still alive, help me put her on her bed then we can be on our way,"

6

Patsy, among the missing

An hour later, Patsy took a sip of her Apple-Spice tea in Dizzy's diner and asked with tears running down her face, "Why is this happening to me? All I want to do is live a normal life like everyone else. But no, everyone and their brothers out to slice me open, and there is nothing in me but my guts,"

Patrick questioned, "Joan said she found you amongst the old runes. Can you remember what you were doing there?"

Gideon motioned for a pen and a sheet of paper then he wrote. I was sitting on Patsy's shoulder as she strolled through the park when two tall men with short light brown hair dressed in dark brown fatigues began to chase us. Patsy held me in her arms and took off running through the park. When we reached the old runes, the two men were almost on top of us. I told Patsy that we had to stand and fight or die trying. I stood in front of Patsy with my Katanas in my paws. But the two men seemed to vanish into thin air. I pointed to a mound of Earth in front of me where Patsy dropped the gold-scrolled key. Then a pile of dirt fell on top of me as Patsy shrieked; I heard a thump, like a body hitting the ground. I then went offline until Joan turned me back on,"

Alexis stated, "The way I see it, Joan dumped dirt on Gideon, then attacked Patsy. Brought her back to her place and dressed her up to look good for the reward money, but Patsy disappeared with the key and her diamond-studded purse,"

Patrick stated, "That explains why Patsy has memory loss. But where do you go, Patsy, when you vanish, and why is the key protecting you?"

Patsy stated, "It's hard to believe Joan was about to kill us when she helped me so much,"

Alexis stated, "Money will cause people to act in ways they normally don't. In Joan's case, sad to say, she is driven by Money,"

Patsy put her arms around Gideon bear, saying, "What is it that you are not telling me? I look at my buddy Gidster and the technology around me, and he is far beyond what the people here can do,"

Alexis stared at her husband, not knowing how to answer Patsy's question.

Patsy then asked, "Just where was the city of Odessa? I know what I read and heard, and a garden flashes in my mind when I hear someone talk about it, but I can't believe that it is on the other side of the galaxy,"

Patrick stated, "There could be life on the other side of this galaxy,"

"Seriously," said Patsy, "The Milky Way Galaxy is 120,000 light-years across. That's 621,371,000,000,000,000 miles, and you're telling me a man can travel that distance in an afternoon. No, I don't think so,"

Patrick smiled sheepishly and said, "We use something called a portal. That's a two-dimensional gateway,"

Alexis stated, "A thousand years ago, on the other side of this galaxy, there were three planets in a solar system, Milichius, Hortensius, and Pharez, with the planet Milichius being the closest to the sun, and Pharez was the last planet in the system. There were two moons in the system: the moon Stadium orbited Pharez, and the other around Milichius. Over ten billion people lived on the three worlds, not including the people who lived on the moon of Stadium. The rulers of Pharez decided to use ion-fusion energy with a new material the scientist had just discovered to create a cheaper form of energy, but the idiots created a chain reaction that destroyed all three planets and sent the two moons hurtling toward the sun. Fortunately, the moons slipped into a safe orbit around the sun but not before the radiation from the explosion saturated the atmosphere of Stadium, condemning everything on it to an agonizing death. The garden where you were assaulted was on the moon of Stadium. Your horse-riding accident was on the planet Pharez. Professor Rollins had a lab in Odessa city where he created you to defeat an advanced computer program, Lucy. She trapped you in a cave, dismantled you, and left you for dead. Teeny found you a thousand years later and reactivated you.

But how you got her on Earth with the lost key of Odessa, Patrick and I can't figure out,"

Patsy stated, "I am still having a hard time believing that my brain is inside a mechanized Robot. True, my legs can come off, but that doesn't mean I am what you call a Mandroid. It's just modern technology for those without limbs,"

"Where did you get a lamebrain idea like that," questioned Patrick.

"Jeff says he is a Mandroid, but his torso is all human. So, I am just like Jeff sort a speak,"

Jeff walked into the diner, spotted Patsy, sat next to her, and put his arm on her shoulder, saying, "There you are, my Cactus Flower. What do you say we find a quiet spot and catch up on our relationship."

Patsy shoved Jeff on the floor, saying, "Get lost, creep."

Gideon stood on the seat with his swords in his paws, waiting for Jeff to make a wrong move.

Jeff went to push Gideon off the seat, but he took a swipe at Jeff with his Katona, nicking his side.

Patrick stated, "If I were you, I'd find another diner to have your coffee because the bear doesn't like you."

"It's a computer-generated image that's malfunctioning, Patsy; turn that thing off so we can talk,"

Gideon hopped on the table, pointed his blade at Jeff, and stared at him. When Jeff went to sit next to Patsy, Gideon did a flip, landing on Jeff's right shoulder, and placed his sword against his throat.

Patsy stated, "Gidster is my protector and if he doesn't like you, then leave if you value your life,"

Jeff took hold of the blade, pressing against his throat to remove it, and discovered Gideon was stronger than he expected. Gideon flipped back on the table and then pointed to the door with his sword.

Jeff muttered, "Stupid bear," and left.

Patsy went to pick up her mug of tea, but her hand passed through it. She took the gold key from her purse, stared at it, and exclaimed, "Oh, Lord, no, not again. The key fell on her seat as she vanished. Patrick picked up the key, saying, "This is not good. The key usually goes with her when she vanishes,"

Alexis suggested, "I say we question Joan to find out what she knows about Patsy and the key,"

"Good idea. Pick up Gideon, and let's go,"

Patrick barged into Joan's home with Alexis behind her and demanded, "Why did you lie to us about Patsy and the key,"

"Get out of my house before I call the cops," shouted Joan, pointing to the door.

Patrick let go of a charge of electricity from his fingertips, sending Joan flying across the living room and onto the floor.

Alexis helped Joan to her feet, saying, "You'd better tell my husband before he turns you into a burned-out cinder,"

Joan shouted, "Have a short circuit," and picked up a glass of water from the coffee table and threw it in his face.

Alexis swung around and belted Joan's jaw with her fist knocking her out cold. stared at her, saying, "I have an idea,"

A short time later, Joan came too bound and gagged, dressed in her beige, two-piece bathing suit, in her hot tub full of mineral oil. Her eyes widened in fear as she gazed at Alexis holding a small pot of flaming mineral oil, thinking she would set the oil in the hot tub on fire with her.

Alexis placed the pot of burning oil on the tub's edge and asked, "What do you know about Patsy and the gold key? And don't give me that line of malarkey that you found her there because I know you didn't,"

Patrick studied Joan for a minute, then approached the hot tub. He took hold of Joan's left arm, pushed it in, then rotated it counterclockwise and removed it. Joan trashed around in the hot tub, trying to escape Patrick.

Alexis hauled Joan out of the hot tub and held her down as Patrick removed her other arm and legs. He yanked down the gag and then asked, "Mandroid, Terrie Joan Ramsey, why are you after Patsy? Please think before you answer my question. Because all I have to do is call 911 and have Earth's paramedics find you like this. Trust me when I say you will spend the rest of your existence being probed by Earth's scientists. Now, why are you after Patsy,"

"How did you know I was a Mandroid,"

"Only a Mandroid's skin will glow when they are soaking in mineral oil, and their bodies do not radiate heat the way a human does."

40

"Patsy was the first one to have a Mandroid body, and Professor Rollins gave just to her special abilities, which the rest of us want,"

Patrick inquired, "Out of the five Mandroids, how many are left,"

Terrie thought for a moment, then said, "There's Tom Marks, who spearheads the attack on Patsy, Jeff Stearns, Patsy Mullens, and me. Alice Birdson's whereabouts are unknown, but Tom is searching for her so she can be a recipient of what's inside Patsy,"

Patrick asked, "Where is Tom Marks hiding,"

"I don't know,"

Alexis stated, "I think you do,"

"I'm telling you the truth; I do not know where Tom is. Now put me back to gather,"

Alexis took a two-inch round silver disk from her purse and said, "Tell me, or I will use this to inflict excruciating pain throughout your body,"

"You're bluffing,"

"Let me put this on your tummy and find out,"

Just as Alexis was about to put the pain-giving device on Terrie's abdomen, she hollered, "Alright! I'll tell you, just don't put that thing on me,"

"Where is he,"

"I'm to meet Tom in front of the granite monolith in the park today at five o'clock,"

Alexis flipped open the silver disk, looked in the mirror to see if her makeup was good then put it in her purse.

Terrie grumbled, "You lied to me. That disk doesn't give pain; it's your makeup mirror,"

"I didn't lie. It gives me pain every time I look into it and see that my face is a mess,"

"Come on, Patrick, we have just enough time to get to the park,"

Terrie shouted, "Hey, how about putting me back together before you leave,"

"Nah," stated Alexis, "This way, you won't run off,"

"Give me a break, will yah," shouted Terrie.

Alexis asked, "Okay, which limb do you want to be broken,"

"Cute, now put me back together," roared Terrie.

Alexis put Terrie's arms back on, slipped a dress on her, then propped her up in the back of Patrick's Blue Ford SUV, with Gideon watching her.

Terrie complained, "Hey, what about putting my legs back on,"

Patrick stated, "You'll get them back when we talk to Tom,"

"If Tom doesn't see me, he won't show,"

In the park, Alexis sat Terrie on the ground, leaned her against the stone column, slipped her legs under her dress so they appeared to be attached, then sat at a picnic table with Patrick a short distance away.

Some five minutes later, a tall man with short black hair clad in a business suit approached Terrie and said, "A nice day for a walk in the park, so what are you doing sitting on the ground."

"Relaxing, Patrick showed up and took Patsy away before I could stop them,"

Tom stated through clenched teeth, "I told you to sedate Patsy when she was in your custody,"

"I didn't have time,"

Tom spotted Patrick and Alexis swiftly approaching and shouted, "You set me up!" He grabbed Terrie by her shoulders, picked her up, and noticed her legs weren't attached. He threw her on the ground, then shoved a knife in her chest and ran off.

Patrick stated to his wife, "Keep pressure on the wound while I get the car,"

At Terrie's home, Alexis lay her on the bed and prepared her for emergency surgery.

Terrie asked, "Am I gonna die,"

"I don't think so, but we'll know more once Patrick looks inside of you,"

"If I die, please take me home,"

An hour and twenty minutes later, Patrick closed the wound on Terrie's chest and let her sleep. He made a pot of Hazelnut coffee, poured Alexis and himself a cup said, "We need to get her off this planet ASAP. Who knows what Tom will do to Terrie now that she has betrayed him,"

"I think it should be soon because while you were sowing up Terrie, I stepped outside and saw three sinister-looking characters checking out the house,"

Patrick tapped his watch and said, "Su, I need a portal at my position right away,"

Seconds later, an eight-foot-tall two-dimensional gateway opened on the far wall of the bedroom. A five-foot-six-foot-tall oriental woman with short black hair clad in frilly, pale blue blouse and dark blue slacks exited the portal and asked, "What's the emergency,"

Patrick greeted Su, pointed to Terrie, and said, "Terrie is a Mandroid and was stabbed in the chest. Do you think you and Calistus could take care of her?"

"Do you know who stabbed her,"

"It's a long story,"

"I have time,"

"Mandroid Patsy Mullen's showed up on Earth with a gold scrolled key with no memory. A Mandroid named Tom is trying to kill her for what's inside her. Terrie worked for Tom to capture her but helped us locate him. Tom stabbed her when he discovered that she had betrayed him. Now we have to get her off this planet before he kills her,"

"That explains the strange signals Cal has been picking up on the surveillance monitor,"

"Can you give me their locations," asked Patrick.

"Terrie Joan Ramsey lives in this house; Tom Marks lives on 15 Ridge Avenue; Patsy Mullens is presently living in this park; Jeff Stearns lives at 20 Red Rock Way, Alice Birdson, lives on 101 Monroe Street, Eureka, Nevada.

Su knelt by Terrie's bed and said, "I'm Su, and I'm going to take you to Moon Base One for treatment,"

"Can you bring me home to HP 5 when I am well?"

"Sure, no problem,"

With Terrie safely on Moon Base One, Alexis picked up Gideon, saying, "Do a scan of the park so we can find Patsy,"

Patrick stated, "Boyd Memorial Park is huge but I'll do my best,"

Some twenty-one minutes later, Patrick spotted Patsy with a few dark gray rags wrapped around her for clothes digging in a garbage can. But took off running for the trees when she spotted them. Alexis shouted, "Patsy, it's Patrick and me!"

Patrick took a small energy pistol out of his pocket, glanced around then fired, stunning Patsy.

7

Walking again

In Terrie's home, Patrick stated, "Alexis, put Patsy in the shower and get her cleaned up; then I'll give her an exam to find out why she can't talk or recognize us,"

An hour later, Patsy, dressed in jeans and a yellow t-shirt, sat at the counter eating her ham sandwich like a wild animal. When Alexis or Patrick approached her, she would put her hands in front of her face and moan.

Patrick gazed at his wife, saying, "I can't find anything wrong with her."

Gideon waddled up to Patsy and raised his paws for her to pick him up. But all she did was stare at him. Alexis picked up the bear and handed him to Patsy. But she moaned and recoiled with her arms covering her face.

Gideon hopped on the counter, slowly approached Patsy, and patted her arm to calm her down.

Patsy slowly took Gideon in her arms, then rocked back and forth.

Alexis inquired, "Where is the key,"

"It's in me medical bag; why,"

"I have a hunch; give it to Patsy,"

Patrick placed the gold key on the counter, then slowly pushed it towards her.

Patsy stared at it for a minute, then picked it up to examine it. The key gave off a yellow glow that enveloped her head for twelve seconds. Patsy smiled, saying, "Lord, I missed you guys so much,"

Patrick asked, "Can you remember anything,"

"I was in the same dark forest running from someone; I felt a sharp pain in my back and passed out. I came too in a lab with wires attached to my head, then everything went black, and I found myself in the park, fearful of everything scrounging for food, unable to speak. It wasn't until the key surrounded my head with a yellow light that my understanding of who you two were, returned,"

A week later, sitting in Patrick's Blue Ford SUV outside the Owl Café in Eureka, Nevada. Patrick pointed to a five foot five inches tall woman with long brown wavy hair clad in a ragged yellow dress, coming out of the café.

Patsy inquired, "Why is Alice in a wheelchair and wearing rags for clothes,"

Alexis quickly exited the vehicle and up to Alice, saying, "Let me push you to where you need to go. Oh, I'm Alexis,"

"I have to pick up a few things at the General Store,"

"Tell me where it is, and I'll push you there,"

In a light blue ranch on 101 Monroe Street, Eureka, Nevada. Alexis helped Alice put away her groceries, then asked, "How did you come to be in a wheelchair,"

Alice hung her head, saying, "It's a long story that I do not want to get into right now,"

Alexis shouted, "You can come in now!"

Patrick, Gideon, and Patsy walked in, and Alexis stated, "This is my husband Patrick and my good friend Patsy and Gideon, the Avenging Bear. They're here to help you,"

"In what way, rob and kill me,"

Alexis stated, "The three of us are from the Planetary Alliance and came to Earth in search of the five Mandroids and why they left the Alliance."

Alice snapped back in anger, "Then the three of you can get out of my house,"

As Alice pointed to the door, she had a difficult time lifting her arm.

Patrick slowly approached her, saying, "You can't hide the fact that this hot, dry weather has dried out your joints and is why you are in a wheelchair,"

"I have no idea what you are babbling about, Shorty,"

Patrick motioned to his wife to shut Alice off and then dismember her,"

Alexis held her hand on Alice's off switch just above her left breast while Patsy removed her limbs, and Patrick went to the SUV for the mineral oil.

After Alexis and Patsy wiped Alice down with the mineral oil and applied a good amount to the joints, they dressed her, left her lying on the bed, and turned off.

An hour later, Alice walked into the living room dressed in a pair of new jeans, a white button-down blouse, and shoes that Alexis had bought her. She slowly scanned the room and said, "It feels so good to walk again; it seems I miss judged you. Let me make a pot of coffee and tell you why us Mandroids left the Alliance,"

A short time later, Alice took a swallow of her coffee and said, "For one, I did not want to be put in this mechanical contrivance. Then along came the Planetary Alliance, promising us everything under the sun. But what we got was the opposite,"

"Can you expound on that, please," asked Alexis.

"I had a beautiful home in the suburbs and a job that was the envy of everyone. Then the backbiting and gossip about me being a robot started, and I was treated like something you scrape off the bottom of your shoe. Then my home began to be pelted with rocks and garbage calling me all kinds of derogatory names. Mandroid Tom told me about a chance to move to Earth. So, I sold everything I owned and gave it to Tom for a chance to start a new life on this planet. The three other Mandroids settled in Oregon, but I wanted to live in Nevada. However, hybrid Patsy Mullins thought she was better than us and refused Tom's offer,"

Patrick stated, "The reason Patsy didn't take Mandroid Tom up on his offer. She knew he was and is a con artist and a thief. He charged the three of you an excessive amount of money to move to Earth so he could live high on the hog while the rest of you scrounged to live. By the way, has Tom contacted you yet,"

Alice took a swallow of her coffee and then stated, "I've received three letters and five e-mails from Tom, all telling me how important it was for me to contact him. But since he took all my money for me to come to this planet, I don't want to speak to him ever again,"

Alexis asked, "Why did you call Patsy a hybrid Mandroid,"

"Professor Rollins gave Patsy the ability to connect to any computer or network so she could take down the advance walking, talking, three-dimensional computer program Lucy. But she failed and was never heard from again," Alice stared at Patsy for a minute, then said, "Waite a minute, your Mandroid Patsy. Did you have a moment of weakness and decided to check out how us poor slobs are doing so you can gloat,"

Patsy lowered her head, saying, "I guess I am a Mandroid, but how I got here and why I can't remember I don't know,"

Alice gave Patsy a friendly hug and then said, "I am sorry for my attitude. Stick with me, kiddo, and you'll be right as rain in no time,"

Patrick asked, "Alice, do you know why Mandroid Tom Marks would want the ability to connect to computers,"

Alice stated, "I remember Tom Marks before he was given a Mandroid body. He was a smooth-talking piece of work and was always in trouble with the law. Just before his accident, he tried to con an old lady out of her hard-earned money. The woman's brother knew what Tom was trying to do and took chase. Tom fell off a cliff and was paralyzed from the neck down. His mother gave Professor Rollins a sob story, and he put Tom's brain in a Mandroid. However, because Mandroids were new, the law protected them. Which gave Tom the freedom to do whatever he wanted,"

Patrick asked, "Did you know Tom is trying to kill Patsy and almost killed Terrie Joan Ramsey, who is recovering from a stab wound on Moon Base One, with Su and Calistus."

Patsy showed Alice the gold scrolled key and asked, "Have you ever seen anything like this,"

Alice held it in her hands, saying, "I don't believe I'm holding the Gold Key of Odessa. But where is the other half,"

"The other half," questioned Alexis.

"Yes, there is a key and lock; the one who has both halves will have great power and be protected from all harm,"

Alice took her thirty-eight revolver from the kitchen drawer and shot Patsy. A yellow aurora instantly formed around Patsy, deflecting the bullets. Alice then said the lock is in Patsy,"

Patrick stated, "I did two scans and there is nothing inside her,"

"Any kind of scan can't detect it. But if Tom gets his hands on both halves, we are in big trouble,"

Then, Tom casually strolled in with a smile, holding a western-style six-shooter in his hand. He slowly scanned the kitchen and said, "You're looking good, Alice, Patsy, if you will kindly come with me, and if you don't, your friends will die. Shorty, don't even think of using that electric charge you have; better yet, everyone take off your shoes and socks, and Patsy, shove their socks in their mouths and use this duct tape their mouths shut; then duct tape their hands and feet,"

Once everyone was tied up, Tom landed a right cross to Patsy's jaw knocking her out. He then took a sharp knife from the drawer to cut her open to find the gold lock. He opened her blouse, and as he touched Patsy's stomach with the knife, a woman's voice said, "Don't even think about it. Drop the knife and slowly stand,"

When Tom turned around, he said, "Well if it isn't Miss Terrie Joan Ramsey back from Moon Base One and I see you've recovered from the knife wound. But that's what one gets when you double-cross someone. Now put down the gun, and let's talk this over,"

Terrie fired a shot, nicking Tom's right shoulder, saying, "That's for stabbing me,"

"You wouldn't shoot an unarmed man, would you,"

"I'm tempted to. But I tell you what, if you can get out of this house in ten seconds, I won't put a bullet in your head,"

With Tom gone, Terrie untied everyone, and Alice listened carefully to Terrie's voice and questioned, "Mandy Fryberger is that you inside that Mandroid,"

"Shhhh, Mandy died a long time ago, and Terrie Joan Ramsey was born,"

Alice asked, "Do you remember what we used to do just about every Saturday night,"

"I still dream about those fun times," stated Terrie,

"So, do I? Hey, do you remember what one guy did after we pulled a prank on him,"

Terrie held her jaw, saying, "I can still feel his fist on my jaw. He hit me so hard,"

"Jaw?" questioned Alice. I thought he cracked two vertebrae in your neck, and you had to wear a neck brace for three months. But why did you leave the church,"

Terrie lowered her head, saying, "That following Sunday, I walked into the church wearing my neck brace and sat in the last seat on the right. After the service, the pastor walked down the center aisle talking to people, and when he got to me, he spoke to a sister on the other side, totally avoiding me. When he did that to me every Sunday, I attended another church,"

"I am so sorry I didn't know that" stated Alice.

Patrick spoke up, saying, "I hate to break up this old home session, but we should be going before Tom returns with some of his goons,"

Later, Patrick was heading north with the others in his SUV when Terrie stated, "Don't look now, but there is a huge black ten-ton dump truck about to run us off the road,"

"I see it," stated Patrick as he stepped on the gas.

The truck rammed the back of the SUV, causing Patrick to swerve back and forth across the road,

Terrie shouted, "I got this!" and spread herself out in the back, pointing her pistol at the driver of the truck. When the truck tried to ram them again, Terrie fired her gun, striking the driver in his forehead. The truck swerved and then flipped over. Terrie shouted Step on it, Shorty!"

Back in Terrie's home in Ashland, Oregon, she showed Alice her hot tub full of mineral oil and said, "Hop in and get rid of that dry skin of yours,"

An excited Alice took off her shoes and jumped in clothes and all, smiled, saying, "You don't know how good this feels,"

Terrie put on a skimpy yellow two-piece bathing suit and stepped in the hot tub, and said, "Judging by your attitude about Tom, I'd say you had a relationship with him,"

Alice growled, "I don't want to discuss that Pond Scum,"

Alexis joined the two women clad in a two-piece dark blue bathing suit and focused her attention on Alice, saying, "You had quite a few chances to break away from Tom, but you didn't. So, the only one you can blame is yourself,"

"How do you know about my past," snapped Alice.

Alexis stated, "You've been walking with the Lord for a long time, and He told you that a relationship with Tom would not work, but you persisted,"

"If you're so smart, what did the Lord tell me," snapped Alice.

"The Lord showed you that you like to travel, Tom doesn't; you have no responsibilities, Tom does. Your, cozen Norman and many others even told you to stay away from Tom, but you wouldn't listen to them even though he hurt you dozens of times,"

"Who have you been talking to," questioned Alice.

"The Lord Jesus loves you and wants you to understand who the blame was for all the hurt you received and will heal you because of the finished work on the cross."

Alice replied in a soft voice, "Forgive me, Lord, it was my fault, not Tom, and forgive me for my anger and bitterness,"

8

Retaliation

Patsy merrily strolled up to the hot tub, swirled her right hand in the warm mineral oil, then questioned, "Alice, your memory of Odessan history is better than anybody I know. Was Odessa really on the other side of the galaxy? Despite what everybody told me, I believe the ancient city of Odessa and the galaxy's garden were somewhere on Earth. One more thing, does the key have the power to transport me someplace else because I keep finding myself in some dark forest running from somebody. This last time I wound up on an exam table in a brightly lit room with wires attached to my head."

Alice stated, "Odessa is definitely on the other side of the galaxy and is in the Planetary Alliance. They travel here by way of a portal, a two-dimensional gateway that opens on the dark side of Earth's moon. The key will protect you and give you power as long as you have its counterpart, the lock, but it can't teleport you anywhere. However, on the dark planet, there is a forest that doesn't let in sunlight. Someone from that forest may have picked up the key's energy signal and teleports you there to locate the other half of the key somewhere inside you. But don't ask me how he is doing it because I don't know."

"But Patrick checked, and the lock is not inside me,"

Alice stated, "Oh, but it is in you because the key keeps protecting you. Most likely put there by the Professor when he put your brain in your Mandroid body,"

"Can you prove it to me,"

"I already did when I tried to shoot you. What more proof do you need besides that,"

Alice got out of the hot tub, took the double-edged sword hanging on the wall, stood in front of Patsy, saying, "I'm sorry I have to do this again," and swung the sword to cut her in two. Instantly, a yellow shield formed around Patsy protecting her. Alice tried three more times with the same results; she then stated, "Now do you believe me,"

"Okay, but what about the key making me powerful,"

Alice dressed, then said, "Come outside with me,"

The two women stood in the back of Patrick's SUV, and Alice stated, "Pick up the car,"

"Are you kidding? It has to weigh at least a ton,"

"To be exact, that SUV weights about five thousand pounds; now pick it up,"

Patsy took hold of the back bumper, and a yellow glow formed around her as she easily picked up the vehicle. She put it down, gazed at Alice with a devilish grin, then said, "Hold that thought until I get back," and walked away.

Some forty-seven minutes later, Patsy entered Loui's restaurant and up to Tom, a tall man in his thirties with black hair table enjoying his Flame-grilled skewers, put her hands on the table, and stated, "You bother me one more time, and I'll turn you into a pile of puke,"

Tom stated, "Get her boys,"

Three burly men with short haircuts, dressed in jeans and white t-shirts, dragged Patsy out back to dismember her. She shook them lose with no problem, then said, "It's time I taught you boys some manners,"

Patsy landed a blow to one man's jaw, shattering it and sending the other two on the ground out cold. Then stood at Tom's table and said, "Is that all you got,"

A shocked Tom asked, "How did you,"

Patsy picked up Tom by her left hand, sat him on top of his food, and said, "I don't ever want to see you or any of your cronies again," and left with a smile of satisfaction on her face.

Back at Terrie's home, Patrick met Patsy happily walking up the driveway and asked, "Don't tell me you went and stomped on Tom,"

With a smile on her face, Patsy stated, "Yes, I stomped on Tom and his three goons,"

Patrick moaned, "That was the last thing you should have done. Now, he's gonna retaliate big time," Patrick shouted, "Okay, everyone, let's pack and get out of here before Tom gets here!"

Just then, Jeff casually strolled in, brandishing his 44 Magnum, saying, "Patsy, you shouldn't have done that to Tom; now, I'm gonna have to punish you,"

"You and what army," asked Patsy.

Jeff pointed his gun at Alice and said, "Since I'm the only one with a gun, I'm all that's needed,"

Patsy stated, "Group hug," then said, "Now try and kill us,"

Jeff stated smiling, "But can that fancy thing of yours protect you against a fire,"

Before Jeff could light the torch, Gideon sliced his leg, causing Jeff to drop the unlit torch. Gideon then attacked Jeff with his sword chasing him out of the house.

A short time later, Terrie stated, "I have a map Atlas just in case the GPS fails; now let's get outta here before something else happens,"

Terrie heard a bang at the front door and went to answer it. She hollered, "Everyone out of the house; a Sherman Tank is coming up the front lawn!"

Some ten minutes later, Jeff crawled out of the tank, stood on the rubble, and said, "That's what, army. Now all I have to do is find Patsy's body and get the other half of the key,"

Suddenly a hand reached up from the debris, grabbed Jeff's left ankle, and hauled him under it with him screaming in terror.

Later, Jeff stood in a protected part of the basement staring at a disheveled Terrie and shouted, "You scared the crap out of me. Warn a body the next time you want to talk. What do you have to report? Have you convinced Alice to join up with Tom and me,"

"Don't worry, they're all out cold, but did you have to demolish my home?"

"You knew what I was going to do and weren't supposed to be in your home when I attacked,"

"I have to admit, faking being dismembered in that forest so you could get on Patsy's good side was clever, and the bogus wedding to Patsy so that you could get information out of her was brilliant. But did you have to be over-friendly with her? The other half of the key is a lock, which is definitely inside Patsy. However, thanks to Alice, Patsy now knows the power she can wheel, so be careful, my love," Terrie gave Jeff a long passionate kiss and then said, "When this is over, you and I are going to a secluded planet and spend months together to get reacquainted,"

Jeff patted Terrie's butt, got in the tank, and drove away.

When Terrie turned around, Alice silently looked at her and asked, "Where are the others? Are they dead?"

"How long have you been standing behind me,"

"About a minute. Who were you talking to,"

"No one. You wanna help me dig out the rest of our group,"

Terrie took a magnet from her purse and slapped it on Alice's shutoff switch, turning her off so she couldn't turn herself back on. Terrie then put a large bandage on the magnet, saying, "I hate to do this to you, but I can't have you telling the group about Jeff and me,"

With everyone rescued, Patsy stared at Alice lying still and asked, "Are you sure there is nothing we can do to turn her back on,"

"I am positive,"

Patrick stated, "Let me check her wound to see how bad it is,"

Terrie quickly said, "She'll be fine in a couple of days; all she needs is rest,"

"I am a doctor, you know, so let me be the judge of her condition,"

"This is or was my home, and I will not let you touch Alice, is that clear," snapped Terrie.

Alexis went to the SUV and returned with a white cloth, made as if she stumbled and fell against Terrie. She put the cloth over Terrie's mouth, and nose putting her to sleep. Alexis smiled at her husband and said, "A little bit of chloroform will do it every time. Now let's see what's wrong with Alice,"

Alice came too after Patrick took off the bandage and magnet, and Alice stated, "Terrie is a double agent,"

Alexis asked, "Where did you get a fool idea like that?"

"I woke when I heard Jeff getting out of the tank and heard him tell Terrie that she was the love of his life. I also found out that Terrie is trying to persuade me to side with him and Tom, but that's not going to happen, not in a million years,"

A curious Alexis questioned, "How do you know Jeff and Terrie are lovers, and she's not just stringing him along,"

Alice grimaced, then said, "The long hot-blooded kiss she gave Jeff told me everything,"

Patrick stated, "Lie back down so I can put the cloth bandage back on you. I don't want Terrie to know we found her out,"

Terrie came too ten minutes later, glanced at Alice, then inquired, "Were to from here,"

Alexis held her stomach, saying, "My stomach is beginning to wonder if my head's been cut off because I haven't had a good meal in too long a time,"

Terrie stated, "The Breadboard is the perfect place to eat. Their eggs Benedict is to die for it is so good,"

"What do we do with Alice," asked Alexis.

Alice slowly sat up, moaning, "What happened? The last thing I remember is the house falling on me,"

Terrie helped Alice to her feet, saying, "That meathead Jeff tried to kill us, but thank the Lord we survived,"

At the Breadboard Restaurant, Patrick ordered the Home Fry meal, Terrie and Alexis ordered the Eggs Benedict, Alice ordered the Greek Omelette, and Patsy ordered The Full House.

With Gideon on her lap, Patsy took a bite of her Blueberry pancakes with a mound of whip cream on them, glanced at Patrick then stated, "The short time I was married to Jeff, we had one steamy love affair. I mean, he couldn't keep his hands off me. One afternoon while cuddling, he told me that you were like a ball and chain he'd rather forget. He told me you were selfish, self-centered, and egotistical, and only thought of yourself and nobody else. To be honest, I don't know why anybody would want to throw away a love muffin like Jeff. Wow."

Trying to stay calm, Terrie stated, "If Jeff is such a love muffin the way you say he is, why did you throw him away,"

"When Jeff tried to kill me, I valued my life more than Jeff, the tiger," Patsy then let go with a low soft growl.

Terrie stared at her plate, quietly eating her food, trying not to get upset as Patsy went on about her steamy love affair with Jeff. Terrie slammed her fist on the table and screamed, "Enough already! You talk as if Jeff is God's gift to women!" Terrie paid for her food, then said, "I'll be in the SUV," and stormed off in a huff.

Alexis smiled and stated, "You enjoyed twisting the knife in Terrie, didn't you,"

"You know it. Now I have to repent about the whopper of a lie I told about Jeff,"

"You mean none of what you said about Jeff is true," stated Alexis.

"None of it,"

"Ever think about becoming a writer or a storyteller? Because you sure know how to spin a good yarn,"

"When I lived in Odessa, I used to entertain the kids with cute short stories. One of the children's favorites was the one about the spider with seven legs,"

Patrick asked, "Has anyone have an idea how we are going to turn things around on Tom and Jeff,"

Patsy stated, "What we need is a mole in Tom's organization, so we know what he is planning,"

Alice stated, "I'll do it, seeing he's been trying to get me to join him,"

Patrick said, "It's gonna have to look convincing because Terrie is smarter than she puts on,"

Alexis rushed outside to see if Terrie was still in the SUV, took Patsy in the restroom, came out ten minutes later, and reported, "Patsy and I thoroughly checked each other for a hidden mic and found none," Alexis glanced at her husband and said, "Come on love muffin I'm gonna check you for bugs,"

Some twenty minutes later, Alexis and Patrick approached Patsy, and Alexis said, "I thoroughly checked hubby, and he's clean,"

Patsy asked, "Alice, how are you going to convince Terry that you want to join up with Tom and the others,"

"I'll hang around Jeff's hunt and let him badger me about me joining up with him for a while; then I'll give in. Prayerfully, he won't get fresh with me like the Last time,"

"The last time," questioned Alexis.

'I don't want to talk about it,"

9

The past

Alice sat on the bank of Bear Creek, listening to the swift-flowing water in Riverwalk Park in Ashland, Oregon. She looked up, saying, "Gracious Heavenly Father, I am thankful for the finished work of the Cross because of it; I stand in your thrown room with my problems. Lord, I do not want to go undercover because Jeff is much like my father, who browbeat me daily. Because of that, I am terrified of people who use shouting to control people. Oh, thank you for sending Patsy to Arizona. I was pretty low and needed to see an old friend to pick me up,"

Tears ran down Alice's cheeks as an almost overpowering assurance flooded her being that she was going to be all right. Alice said, "Okay, Lord, I'll do it at your command."

Later, Alice sat at a small square table in Noble Coffee Roasting, nervously nursing her Hazelnut coffee. Terrie sauntered in, ordered a black coffee, sat at Alice's table, and said, "I know how committed you are to helping Patsy, she then dumped a small bag of assorted gems on the table, saying, "I also know that you are in desperate need of money. Help Tom, Jeff, and I get the key from Patsy, and there will be a lot more gens in your pocket,"

Alice pushed the gens away from her, saying, "No, thank you,"

Terrie pushed the gems back to Alice, saying, "Jeff and Tom want to help mankind with both halves of the key. But Patsy only wants the power it gives her, not help the poor and outcast."

"I said no, now leave me alone," and pushed the gems to Terrie.

Terrie stared at Alice for a minute, then stated, "I can always let it be known that you sided with Jeff, but I won't,"

"I wish I could go back in time and kick Harold's butt for dropping that boulder on me,"

Terrie smiled, saying, "With both halves of the key, you can,"

Alice's eyes lit up as she asked, "You are kidding,"

"With the key, anything is possible,"

Alice grabbed the gems saying, "Sounds great. Who do I have to kill,"

Terrie stated, "To prove your loyalty, I want you to kill Alexis,"

"Why her?"

" She's a pain where I sit because she's always pulling practical jokes on people,"

Alice called Alexis and said, "Come to where I am, and let's talk. I buy the coffee," She ended the conversation and said, "Alexis will be here in ten minutes,"

Alexis entered the coffee shop seven minutes later and greeted Alice with a hug. She staggered backward with a knife in her chest and a look of shock on her face as she fell to the floor.

Terrie stared at a bloody Alexis with a knife in her chest and said, "Let's get out of here!"

Later in the back of the ambulance, Alexis sat up, looked at the two female paramedics, and said, "Thanks, guys. Now help me take this fake chest off,"

One paramedic inquired, "How does it work?"

Alexis held the false woman's chest in her hands and pushed the knife into it, saying, "The woman's fake boobs and stomach easily slips over my head. And when someone hits the right spot, the knife pops out, splattering blood all over me, so it looks like I've been stabbed,"

The other paramedic asked, "Alexis, have you ever thought about seeing a shrink? Because you are one sick puppy,"

The paramedic handed Alexis a knapsack and asked, "How are you going to keep them from finding out that you are still alive?"

Alexis opened the knapsack and took out extra padding to change her from a B cup to a D. Gave herself bigger ears and a pug nose and changed the size and shape of her chin. She then put on Jeans and a red sweatshirt. Then asked the paramedics, "What do you think?"

They gave her their okay and let her off at the next corner. Alexis called Patsy and asked, "Can you pick me up? I'm at 2 Grisham Street, Thanks,"

Some ten minutes later, Patsy pulled her car to the curb, got out, and looked for Alexis but couldn't find her. Ten minutes later, Patsy was about to get in her car and drive away when Alexis tapped her left shoulder, saying, "Looking for me?"

Patsy spun around, stared at the strange woman, and asked, "Alexis?"

"Alexis was stabbed to death by Alice; I'm Cyndy Winters,"

Patsy smiled, saying, "Get in the car and fill me in on the way back to the house,"

"House, what house?" asked Alexis.

A middle-aged couple is letting us stay in their late mother's multi-level home on Morton Street."

Patrick approached his wife in the house and said, "I wonder about you sometimes."

Alexis gave her husband a kiss saying, "Practical jokes are my way of dealing with my past,"

"I was concerned you weren't coming back to me because Jeff stabbed you."

Alexis held Patrick's hand, saying, "I think we need to go for a walk,"

In the kitchen, Patsy held the gold key in her hand, saying, "I wish I could go back in time and," she paused and thought, "*If I prevent myself from having that accident, I won't be here now,*" Patsy then stated, "Key, take me to Professor Rolland's Lab a thousand years ago," But nothing happened. She put the key in her purse, took two steps, and heard a man say, "Patsy, what are you doing here?"

She spun around, hollered, "Professor!" and gave him a long hug.

He took her to a corner of his lab, lifted a white sheet, and said, "Patsy, meet your Mandroid. The Professor then stated, "The only reason you are here is you found the gold key, and somebody is after it,"

"Those somebodies are your Mandroids, Jeff, Terrie, and Tom, who want to kill me and remove the other half of the key,"

Patsy studied the Mandroid lying on an operating table, looked at the Professor, and said, "Then it is true I am a Mandroid. I traveled a thousand years back in time to ask you not to put the other half of the key inside me. Because I am tired of people trying to kill me for it."

"The other half of the key is what makes you special and will prevent Lucy from killing you."

Patsy hung her head and said, "I failed to shut Lucy down. She caught me in a cave, stripped me, and dismantled me where I lay for a thousand years. Teeny found me, and Thor and his team helped Lucy turn for the good,"

The Professor stated, "If I don't put the other half of the key inside you, Lucy will surely kill you in the cave," he then stated, "The legend says that the other half of the key is a lock,, but it isn't. The other half is a device six inches square by two and a half inches thick. The key is the power source and slips inside the device to activate it. The device will power up one-fourth of its strength if the key is within two or three feet. Once the key is inside the device, There's no telling what it can do. Jeff, Tom, and Terry can try to kill you all they want, but as long as you have both halves of the device, it will protect you,"

The Professor took a knife from off the table and went to stab Patsy, but he couldn't because of an invisible force field.

Patsy inquired, "Could you open me up and put the key in the device? This way, no one will be able to steal it."

Much later, Patsy woke in a pink nightshirt, lying on a bed in a bedroom of the Professor's home. A short woman in her mid-thirties clad in a deep red dress with a black belt entered the room and gave Patsy a glass of water, saying, "I see you are awake. I'm Sally, the Professor's wife,"

Patsy drank the water, then asked, "Why do I feel dizzy and weak,"

"It will take a few days to get used to the key being inside you,"

Sally gave Patsy a pair of red slacks and a white blouse, then helped her sit in a comfortable chair on their back patio. The Professor sat on her left and said, "You're going to be fragile and woozy for a few days, then you'll begin to feel stronger. But be careful because no one knows what that device will do once it's activated,"

Some three days later, Patsy disguised herself with a blonde wig and some makeup so she wouldn't be recognized. Sat at an outdoor restaurant enjoying her barbecued steak, mashed potatoes with dark brown gravy, and green beans. A short scruffy looking man in his mid-twenties sat at her table and introduced himself as Jeff Sterns.

Patsy thought, *"The Guy's a slob, and he looks nothing like his Mandroid. It's time I had some fun and pumped him for information,"*

Jeff took her right hand and kissed it, saying, "Where have you been all my life, you gorgeous hunk of a woman,"

Patsy yanked her hand away and wiped it with her napkin, saying, "Avoiding you,"

Jeff asked, "What do you say we get together someplace quiet for a cup of tea?"

"So, I can have a little one in nine months; no, thank you." Patsy then asked, "Have you ever heard about the legend of the gold key?"

"I sure have; Tom, Terrie, and I plan to have an accident, so Professor Rollins will give us each a Mandroid the way he plans to give that weirdo Patsy one. That will give us centuries to look for the gold key and the lock."

"What will you do with it once you have it?"

"Destroy everyone and anyone who gets in our way of success. We'll tell everyone that we are using it for the good of mankind, but that is a coverup for our real purpose,"

Patsy stared at Jeff and asked, "The key will give you that much power? What if somebody tries to kill you for it?"

Jeff stated, smiling, "The one who has the key will be invincible,"

"So, the three of you will rule the world,"

"Pretty much,"

Just then, a tall thin woman with short curly lithe brown hair stopped at the table, gave Jeff a kiss saying, "Supper at my place at seven,"

Jeff asked, "Is everything ready,"

The woman replied, "Professor's Mandroid checks out, and he plans to put Patsy's brain in it in two days," then walked away.

Patsy asked, "Who was that poor starving creature, and how does she know what the professor's plans are,"

"That was my wife-to-be Terrie Joan Ramsey, and she works in Professor Rollins's lab,"

Patsy smiled devilishly and said, "What do you say we go to the garden of Pharez? It's only a short hop away,"

A brief time later, in the garden of Pharez. Patsy led Jeff to a secluded place and said, "Go behind that huge orange bush and get ready to snuggle; I'm shy and have to get ready by myself,"

When Patsy saw Jeff's clothes on the bush, she caught a guard's attention by saying, "There is something weird going on behind that bush," Then she quickly hid and watched Jeff be arrested for indecent exposure.

As Patsy was merrily strolling back to Professor Rollins's home. She saw a tall, burly man harassing a woman. Patsy marched up to the man and said, "The woman doesn't want a kiss from you, so bug off Creep,"

The man took hold of Patsy's shoulders, saying, "How about if we get to know each other better,"

Patsy muttered, "Key online," picked the man up by his shirt with one hand, said, "Back off," and threw him five feet. The man sprang to his feet and charged Patsy. She jumped over him, grabbed the back of his shirt and flipped him high in the air, caught him, and slammed him against a nearby wall. He sprang to his feet and charged her again. Patsy landed a hard right cross to his jaw that knocked his feet out from under him. As he lay on the ground unconscious, Patsy asked the woman, "Are you alright?"

The woman replied, "I'm okay, but how did you get so strong,"

"Daily exercise, Hey, let me help you with your groceries,"

When Patsy entered Professor Rollins's home, he was talking to a stout man named Tom. She approached him and asked, "By any chance would your last name be Marks?"

"Why yes, it is. Have we met before?"

"No, we haven't,"

Tom asked, "How about you and I grab a bite at the local restaurant? I would like to talk to you about something,"

Tom ordered a coffee and a tartlet at the restaurant, while Patsy just had black Lemon tea. Tom took a bite of his pastry, then asked, "How would you like to live forever,"

Patsy put on a fake smile and said, "You have my attention,"

Tom stated, "The Professor has a new invention called a Mandroid which he will test out on that loser Patsy. I was hoping you could use your femininity to persuade the Professor to put Jeff, Terrie, and me in

Mandroid bodies. Once he does that, we will spend our energy looking for the lost Key of Odessa,"

"So, you can take over the world; I'll think about it. Now, if you will excuse me, I have to be going,"

As Patsy walked out of the restaurant, she thought, *"Now to put some mistrust in Terrie's mind for Jeff,"*

Patsy staked out Terrie's home and waited for her to leave. When she did, Patsy followed her for several blocks, caught up to her, and said, "Terrie Joan Ramsey, I presume,"

"Yes, what do you want,"

"Stay away from my Jeff if you know what's good for you,"

"If you are implying that Jeff is cheating on me, you are so wrong, lady,"

"Am I? Then how do I know that Jeff snores loud enough to wake the dead? If I am lying, I wouldn't know about the scar on his left butt cheek and that he walks in his sleep. Shall I go on?"

Terrie silently glared at Patsy, then said, "If you will excuse me, I have a few things to do before this evening," Terrie then walked away, but three feet from Patsy, she turned, pointed at her, saying, "You are the woman Jeff was sitting with this afternoon,"

Patsy smiled, waved, turned, and walked away.

10

The one behind it all

Patsy stated at the Professor's home, "I need all the information you have on the Key. If this thing is inside me, I want to know all about it."

The Professor stated, "In the den, on the top shelf on your left is a scroll with all the information concerning the Key and the mythology surrounding it. When you go back to your time, take the scroll with you because I don't want it in my home."

Patsy inquired, "What would happen to me if I had the device removed?"

"Your organs in your body would move back into position, and you wouldn't be as strong, but that's all. If you are thinking about destroying the device, you have my blessing."

Patsy bid goodbye to the Professor and his wife, opened a rift in time and entered. In a fraction of a second, Patsy was standing in the exact spot when she left.

Alexis rushed into the kitchen and asked, "Did you see that bright flash of light?"

"That was me returning from the past with a scroll containing all the information about the key."

Alexis took the scroll, saying, "This is the Odessan key scroll? Far out! Give me a few minutes, and I'll tell you what it says,"

"Buts it's written in Russians,"

"My grandmother was Russian, and my grandfather was Scottish, so Rushen is my second language,"

Patsy took a long hot shower, put on her long green fuzzy robe, and entered the den with its modern furniture; she saw Alexis sitting in a comfortable green recliner, busy reading the scroll, and asked, "What have you found out so far?"

Alexis took off her black reading glasses and said, "It says about twelve hundred years ago on Earth, a group of Russians were digging in some old ruins and came across a gold box with a key in it and accidentally opened a portal to the Pharos solar system. When they saw how warm the planet was, twenty-five hundred people from Earth migrated there and founded the city of Odessa. News about the new technology had spread rapidly to the other planets, and five years later, Odessa was a thriving metropolis. The box and Key are an alien computer with all kinds of futuristic conveniences. Like a hover platform, virtual reality TV and communications, and a road material that would last for centuries. Because of the Key, they were able to create an energy collector in the form of a huge tree and storage cells to store the energy. However, whoever possesses the Key and box has unlimited power and will be protected from all harm,"

Patsy thought for a minute, then stated, "Key, create an exact holographic image of Alexis.

A duplicate of Alexis appeared in front of her in a fraction of a second. She stared at it with her mouth open in shock, then said, "How about putting some clothes on her, a, me before some guy comes in and sees me like that,"

Patsy stated, "Key, dress her,"

Instantly Alexis's copy was dressed in a Russian multi-colored long dress with open shoulders called a sarafans, and a fur coat called a shuba,"

Alexis stated, "Russian fashions one thousand years ago left something to be desired. The joke is over, so how about getting rid of me or it,"

Patsy stated, "Key, get rid of Alexis,"

The real Alexis suddenly vanished, and Patsy quickly hollered, "Key, reverse that statement!"

A drenched Alexis suddenly appeared and said, "Whoa, that was weird; one minute I was talking to you, than I was standing in the middle of Bear Creek. Will you please choose your words carefully because I don't want to wind up downtown Ashland wearing only a smile,"

For the next hour, Patsy tried everything she could think of to remove the holographic image of Alexis but wound up making it solid. Alexis placed it in the corner of the den and called her, Doubleganger.

Patsy inquired, "Where is Patrick?"

"He's around here somewhere. Hey, did I show you the project I am working on in the basement,"

"No, you didn't,"

While Alexis and Patsy were in the cellar, Patrick walked in the den, saw his wife standing in the corner, and asked, "Nice outfit. Do you want to go out to eat for supper,"

But Alexis remained silent; Patrick stared at what he thought was his wife and said a little stronger, "Do you want to eat out this evening,"

With still no response from his loving wife, Patrick asked, "What did I do that you are giving me the silent treatment?"

Alexis entered the den seven minutes later and saw Doubleganger on the floor with Patrick franticly ministering CPR.

Alexis quietly crept up behind him and said in a soft voice, "I love you, my Bug-a-boo,"

Patrick stopped, looked up with tears in his eyes, saying, "I love you me Firefly and am so sorry I wasn't there to save you,"

Alexis gently tapped his right shoulder, saying, "I'm right behind you,"

Patrick sprang to his feet, spun around, looked at his wife, then at Doubleganger on the floor, then at his wife again, and passed out. Patrick came too twelve minutes later, lying on the couch with Alexis applying a cold, wet cloth to his forehead. He sat up quickly and threw his arms around Alexis, saying, "You gave me heart failure, lying on the floor like that,"

Alexis shouted, "You can bring her in now!"

Patsy wheeled Doubleganger in wearing roller skates and said, "I accidentally made a duplicate of your wife, and that's who you saw in the den, Sorry,"

Patrick got off the couch, examined Doubleganger, and said, "Put her in a closet, so I don't mistake her for you. But I have an idea how to stop Tom and Jeff from bothering you, Patsy. Make a duplicate of yourself, and at the right time, we'll set the trap."

"Sounds good to me," stated Patsy, "But Patrick, please leave the room so I can do it."

"Why? Is there some strange way you have to create her that you don't want me to see,"

"My double won't be dressed, and I don't want you to see me like that,"

After Patrick left, Patsy stated, "Key, make a double of me with flexible joints and soft, warm skin,"

An exact duplicate of Patsy appeared in front of her in a fraction of a second, then collapsed on the floor. Alexis knelt and touched its shoulder, saying, "Wow, you won't believe it, but she's soft and warm. Why don't we call her Softie?"

Softie stood to her feet and said, "I am a mechanical contrivance to act and be identical like the humanoid Patsy Mullens,"

"Patsy quickly said, "Alexis, get Softie something to wear before Patrick sees her like that,"

Once Softie was dressed like Patsy, she had Softie greet Patrick while Alexis and Patsy secretly watched. A half-hour later, Patsy walked into the kitchen and said, "Meet Softy Mullens, my twin sister,"

A shocked Patrick stated, "But Patsy, you don't have a twin,"

"I do now, thanks to the key,"

"This is not what I wanted you to make, but she'll have to do. Come on, Softie, I have to give you a physical to see how human you really are,"

An hour later, Patrick entered the kitchen with Softie and said, "Give her something to eat,"

Patsy gave Softie a mug of hot coffee to see what she would do. She put the mug to her lips and said, "This is hot. Do you mind if I wait until it is cool?"

When the coffee was cool, Patsy, Alexis, and Patrick watched Softie drink her coffee, then eat the last jelly donut on the plate.

Patrick stated, "Softie can mimic a human woman in every way. Now for the final test. Call Jeff and tell him that you want to talk to him at Bear Creek,"

Later, Jeff approached Bear Creek, saw what he thought was Patsy, and placed his hand on the small of her back to say hi. Softy spun around, flipped him on his back, and said, "Don't touch me there ever again,"

A shocked Jeff stood to his feet and asked, "What's with the hostility?"

"How else am I to treat you after the way you and your friends have tried to kill me,"

"All we want is that useless gold key you carry in your purse and the lock inside you,"

"I don't have any key in my pocketbook. If you don't believe me, check for yourself,"

After Jeff searched Softie's purse he asked, "Where is the key," he then took what looked like a small cell phone from his right pants pocket, waved it in front of Softie, and questioned, "Where is it?"

"Where is what,"

"What did you do with the key and the other half that's supposed to be in your intestinal area, and it's not there,"

"How do you know where it is in me when it can't be scanned,"

"Tom found a way to scan it; now, where is it, and why did you want to see me?"

"I don't have what you are looking for and am tired of being hounded night and day, so stop it, or I'll go back in time and erase your miserable hide."

Alice approached Jeff, clad in hot pants and a halter top, kissed Jeff, and asked, "Do you know how much I love you?" Alice then gave Jeff a long passionate kiss then whispered, "Let me butter up to Patsy, Alexis, and the others so we'll know their every move,"

"Go for it, Sweet Cheeks," stated Jeff and left.

When Jeff was gone, Alice fell to her knees with the dry heaves; she then jumped into the creek and thrashed around, trying to get rid of the dirty feeling.

Softie waded in the water, put her arm around Alice, and said, "You are going to be alright."

A short time later, the two women sat on the riverbank, and Alice stated, "Being around Jeff made me sick to my stomach, but I had to do it so we could know what they were up to. So, I became Jeff's woman in every sense of the word,"

Softie asked, "What is really bothering you about Jeff,"

"I've known Jeff when we were back in Odessa, and he was a pain where I sit back then. I would send him a daily video gram telling him how sweet and kind he was, and he would never reply. But God forbid if I didn't respond to one of his. When I went to church on Sunday, he would act as if he didn't know me, but Jeff was eager to go out on a date with me. However, if we went out to eat, he would bolt the door before I could stand. He hurt me so much that I left the Christian fellowship group because I felt unwanted,"

Softie stated, "In other words, Jeff was bosom buddies when he was alone with you. But didn't want to admit he was your close friend in public,"

"Yeah, how did you know,"

"Jeff doesn't trust you and let it be known at your Christian group. That's why you felt unwelcome there."

The truth Softie spoke made Alice stare at her with her mouth open as her stress vanished. Alice said, "Thank you, you put to rest a lot of things that had me puzzled about Jeff for years."

Alice carefully studied Softie for a minute, then said, "There is something different about you, Patsy, but I can't quite put my finger on it,"

Back at the house, Alice entered, gave everyone a warm hug then said, "We need a group meeting as soon as possible because I have disturbing news about Tom, Jeff, and Terrie,"

Patrick questioned, "How bad can it be?"

Patsy slowly walked into the room, waved at Alice, and said, "I see you have met my twin, Softie,"

Alice stated, "I knew there was something different about the Patsy who I met at Bear Creek,"

Patsy stated, "The meeting of the Mandroids will come to order, Alexis what are the minutes from the last meeting,"

"There are none,"

Patsy stated, "Any new business,"

Alice stood and said, "Since Terrie has been telling them everything, we have to develop a new way of doing things. But what is important is to divide then conquer."

Patsy stated, "When I was in the past, I set a wedge of mistrust between Terrie and her lover Jeff. We need to work on putting more jealousy between them by portraying Terrie as a femme fatale. Alice, what are Tom and Jeff up to? I know they plan to use the Key to take over the world."

"Tom says he will use the Key to help himself to all the money he wants by creating a portal into any bank vault. Then when he has the funds he needs. He'll invest in the stock, so he has the controlling shears in companies that have a great influence in America; the rest of his plan is too gruesome to mention,"

Softy stated, "There is something missing in this whole scenario. If you'll pardon my language, there's not enough emotional strength in a human that will drive him after something for over one thousand years. He would have given up in discouragement after a few decades. Tom Jeff and Terrie might have started out to look for the Key, but I guarantee you their desire for wealth and power didn't last more than two decades when they didn't find it. Someone in the present has kindled that long-dead fire within them,"

"But who," questioned Patsy.

Alexis stared at Alice and asked, "You've been with that bunch of traitors for two weeks. Who is the top man, number one, the big Cheese,"

Alice stared at the floor for a minute before saying, "Jeff and Terrie are pawns in the seam of things. Tom goes into his room every day at about three in the afternoon and talks to someone. I know he isn't making a cell phone call because he never takes it with him."

Softie asked, "Have you ever listened in on the conversation?

"Yes, Tom calls him Sir, and he uses a Tyrus communicator with an interstellar interphase. I know because I saw him put the communicator under his mattress."

"In English, please," stated Patsy.

"In other words, Tom made an interstellar call. I snuck into his bedroom, checked his communicator, and Tom made a call to the Planet Lazartra,"

Patrick moaned, "If it's true, then Earth is in big trouble."

Patsy stated, "Maybe They're curious about the device,"

Alexis said, "A Lazartran is a lizard in human form and lives in the murky swamps of Lazartra. Their green flesh is slimy, and they are referred to as slime heads. A Lazartran smells like swamp water and will do anything underhanded. General Lars was the worst of them all,"

Alice stated, "I'm not sure, but I think Tom was speaking to General Lazs.

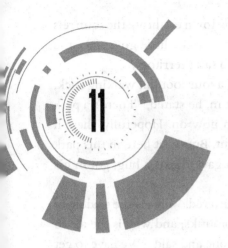

11

The truth revealed

Alexis gave her husband a peck on his cheek, then said, "I'm gonna go for a walk. Be back in a while,"

Sometime later, Alexis was passing a park and saw a man sitting on a bench with a brown bag of peanuts in his hand with tears in his eyes. She sat on his right and asked, "Are you alright?"

"I'll be fine. I just miss my little friend, George,"

"Was he your pet?"

"No, a few years back, I walked across this field full of squirrels, thankful I could walk again, and stood under that tree with the red sign on it and was pelted with acorns. I looked up at the squirrel and stated, "If you don't stop throwing your nuts at me, I'm gonna come up there and kick your little furry butt," The little fella scampered down the tree, stood three feet in front of me as if to say go ahead and try. I smiled and said, "Hey George, meet me at that park bench tomorrow, and I'll give you some nuts," Then, every day for the next year, I sat here and watched George and all his friends chase each other and look for food. One little fella was scurrying across a limb, jumped to the branch on the next tree, and missed. The little guy landed spread eagle on the ground and lay motionless, which led me to believe that he died. He suddenly picked his head up, looked around as if to say hey, I'm alive and scurried off. Today I was prepared to feed George and his little friends, but they're gone; every last squirrel in this park has vanished. The stillness of this field screams a silence, and tragedy happened here that caused the strange disappearance of all the squirrels. But what was it?" Did the town eradicate the squirrels because they thought they were vermin, or did the little guys since the disaster was about to strike and move on to safer territory,"

The old man struggled to stand, using a four-foot-tall walking stick, and made his way to his car. Before he got in, he stated, "There's a park with a pond across town I will visit from now on. Hopefully, there'll be some of God's creatures scurrying about. But to sit here in this park devoid of life is too depressing," The man gave Alexis a hug, got in his car, and drove away.

Alexis slowly scanned the field and muttered, "This is the middle of summer, but where are the birds and chipmunks, and why is the air so still?" Alexis called Patrick on her smartphone and said, "We have to get out of town now!"

"What's wrong, me, Firefly?"

Ashland is about to be his with a disaster, and I, for one, do not want to be here when it strikes! Pick me up in the park just north of you,"

Some sixty-four miles east of Ashland, the group stopped at Nibbley's Café on Washburn Way in Klamath Falls, Oregon. They sat in brown wicker chairs on the cement patio surrounded by colorful flowers. Alexis ordered the Crunchy chicken salad with Almonds, tomatoes, cheddar cheese, bacon bits, and crunchy chicken that sat on a bed of lettuce and green iced tea. Patrick ordered the Ruben, a delicious lean corned beef on grilled rye, topped with sauerkraut Swiss cheese that came with coleslaw and cross-cut fries, and coffee. While Patsy, Alice, and Softy chose the Southwest Philly Wrap, which had Cream Cheese, Bell Peppers, Onions, Tomato, and Steak, served in a hot Tortilla with Salsa and coffee.

While they were eating, a *woman* who was five feet, five inches, in her mid-thirties, with very curly red hair and freckles rushed up to Softy and said, Hi Patsy," she then glanced at Patsy sitting on the other side of the table and said, "Ahhhhh, That's a good one Alexis, who did you get to play the other Patsy,"

Alexis smiled and said, "Hi Cherry, I can't take the credit for this one. The one you thought was Patsy is Softie, a duplicate made by the Key inside of Patsy sitting over there. What brings you and Thor to Earth?"

Cherry ordered a cup of coffee, sat next to Softie, and said, "Calistus of Moon Base 1 told us you guys were staying in Ashland and a mile-wide tornado leveled the town, and we were concerned,"

Alexis stated, "When I noticed that the wildlife had fled the area, so did we."

Cherry asked, "Did you guys forget someone,"

Alice said, "No, we're all here,"

Cherry placed Gideon on the table and said, "Gideon contacted Moon Base 1 that he was left behind. Fortunately, Callistus was able to pull him out before disaster struck,"

Alexis inquired, "Wait a minute. How was Gideon able to contact Moon Base One when he has no mouth to talk,"

"Gideon has an emergency subroutine written in his software that will activate when he is in distress,"

Patrick took a swallow of his coffee and stated, "General Lars is spearheading the attack on Patsy because he wants the power the key will give him and is using Mandroid Tom, Jeff and Terrie."

Cherry stated, "The Lazartrans have found a way to hide their stale pond water smell, attach arms and limbs to get people to think they are a human Mandroid. So, it is possible that one of the Mandroids here on earth is a Lazartran,"

Patsy quickly stated, "It's Jeff,"

Patrick stated, "I did a medical scan on Jeff, and it came up inconclusive, but he is definitely not a Mandroid,"

Cherry stated, "Noleck of the grays, Commander of the time saucer ship, Cassiopeia, is looking for a computer lost in one of their time travel expeditions. If you hear anything, let Thor know so we can return it to him. Hey, gotta go,"

Patsy stated, "Jeff can't be one of the lizard people because I went back in time, and I can confirm it is definitely Jeff. But when I was married to him, he didn't act like a Mandroid,"

Alice piped up, saying, "I was Jeff's woman for several weeks, and he is not human. Because one day the temperature dropped and Jeff became sluggish as if he were cold-blooded,"

Just then, a tattered Jeff staggered up to Patsy and said, "You gotta help me."

Patsy gave him some of her food then he stated, "Someone by the name of General Lars had me tied up in his house and had someone posing as me."

Patrick scanned Jeff with his medical scanner and said, "He is definitely a Mandroid.

Alice called Jeff on her smartphone and said, "Hey, Sugar Lips. I'm just checking in, and things are quiet; we had to go east because of the storm. How's by you?"

"We hunkered down until after the storm; you say put until we can get there."

Alice ended the call and said, "I just talked to Jeff on the phone,"

Patrick made a call on his watch, saying, "Moon Base 1, this is Patrick. I have someone to transport up from my position." Patrick took tattered Jeff into the men's room, then came out three minutes later, alone and asked, "Where is Patsy,"

"She's in the lady's room," stated Alice. Some twenty minutes later, Softie went into the women's room to find out what was keeping Patsy. She returned a minute later, saying, "Patsy is gone."

Patrick contacted Moon Base 1 and said, "Calistus, Patsy has disappeared again. Can you get a fix on her?"

"I'll do my best, but who knows where the Key took her,"

Alice stated, "I was the mole the last time and almost puked my guts out being around that creep, Jeff."

Softie saw the distressed expression on Alice's face and said, "I'll do it; just tell me where and when,"

A waitress walked up to the table then said, "You people look like you could use a place to stay. A KOA campground not too far from here has trailers for rent."

Alice stated, "Thank you. We left Ashland just before the tornado hit and are looking for a place to stay."

"If you don't mind me asking, "How did you know It was coming when it struck without warning,"

"When I saw that, the animals were gone, and the air was still and quiet. I knew something was about to happen, so we headed east as fast as possible."

In the KOA campground, Patrick rented a trailer for him and his wife and one for the women.

Softie chased the women out, dressed in a long, low, cut black dress, then greeted Jeff with a smile. Then said in a soft voice, "Hi sexy, how about we have dinner then snuggle for the rest of the evening,"

A delighted Jeff stated, "Can we skip the meal?"

"I made a pork roast, your favorite,"

Thinking Softy was Patsy, Jeff approached her from behind, put his arms around her, saying, "It's been way too long since you've been in my arms,"

Softie stated, "Look, this poor pig gave his life just so you could have this fabulous meal; now eat,"

As Softie was serving Jeff, she turned on the AC and kept sneaking it down a little at a time until Jeff staggered to the couch and passed out. Softie called Patrick so he could take a blood sample, then a short time later, Patrick stated, "Jeff is definitely a cold-blooded Lazartran," Patrick looked at Softie and inquired, "Did Jeff suspect that you were not Patsy,"

"As far as Jeff is concerned, he had dinner with Patsy,"

Alexis rushed out the door, coming back seven minutes later with a pair of her pink silk panties, and tucked them in Jeff's back pocket.

Alice asked, "Softie, while you were eating, was Jeff quiet?"

"He never said a word; why,"

"When Jeff is quiet during mealtime, he suspects something. Softie, meet me in the bedroom so we can change clothes. I want to take your place, and I don't have a sexy black dress,"

With everyone gone, Alice put some of her lipstick on Jeff, took off his shirt, shoes, and socks, then opened his pants, covered him with a blanket, then took hold of his pant legs, and pulled them off. She then turned off the AC and opened the door to let in the heat. Then knelt on the floor by the couch and placed her head on his chest.

Jeff opened his eyes and brushed Alice's hair with his hand saying, "What happened to Patsy, and what are you doing here?"

"You know Patsy, here one minute and gone the next. I came by and found you on the couch, so do you mind if I fill in for her? I'm ready when you are," stated Alice, and placed her hands on her dress as if she were going to take it off.

Jeff stared at Alice for a few seconds, then said, "Seeing you are undercover, let's dispense with sex because I don't want Patrick or the others to suspect that you are a double agent,"

As Alice assisted Jeff in getting dressed, she gave him a long passionate kiss, then rubbed his bare back, asking, "Are you sure you have to go because I was looking forward to spending some quality time with you,"

"I've stayed longer than I wanted to, but when this is all over, we should get together for a long weekend on a deserted planet,"

Alice gave Jeff another long kiss before he walked out the door.

With Jeff gone, Alice ran into the bathroom, dopped to her knees in front of the toilet, and puked her guts out, thinking, "*That guy is the most nauseating person in the Galaxy, and I pray I don't have to deal with him again,*"

A few minutes later, Alexis knelt on Alice's right and said, "I'll get you something for your stomach,"

A short time later, Alice drank the Maalox, then leaned against the bathtub. Alexis sat on Alice's left on the floor and stated, "Did I ever tell you the time I went out on my first date? I had just turned nineteen when this guy where I worked wanted to take me to a swanky restaurant. I put on my fancy blue dress and had my hair permed, but I didn't know what to do about my nervous stomach. The chicken cordon Bleu was out of this world, and of course, Chuck ordered the Baked Alaska, which impressed me tremendously. He then drove to a quiet spot in the park and asked if I wanted to make out. I knew the end results of making out would be us in the back seat of his car with our clothes off. With no way out of the predicament, I let him kiss me. As he got to second base, my stomach erupted all over his new white shirt and he smiled graciously. I was about to apologize when I threw up in his lap. I looked at him sheepishly, then said, "I'll call a cab, and thank you for a wonderful evening. Can I ask you what it about Jeff that turns your stomach,"

"He always was a pain where I sit, but this fake Jeff, there is an aroma about him that is nauseating,"

Alexis stared at Alice, saying, "You dated Jeff back in the Odessa era, didn't you,"

Alice stated, "Let me put it this way. I was in your shoes on my first date. But we went for a walk after dinner, and I didn't lose the contents of my stomach when we kissed and had a miscarriage some months later, and all Jeff did was give me the silent treatment,"

Alexis stated, "I am sorry you had that happen to you. But receive your healing through the finished work on the Cross of Christ and forgive the boy who did it to you,"

12

A tight squeeze

Patsy opened her eyes in a sterile, white room strapped to a gurney, with just a white sheet covering her. She glanced to her left at her clothes thrown on a stainless-steel table and wondered if some guy sexually abused her.

Some six and a half minutes later, a man clad in white hospital garb entered, looked at her, and asked, "What are you doing awake when I injected a sedative in your arm ten minutes ago."

Patsy smiled, saying, "That stuff never works on me; now, if you will remove these strapped holding me to this table and join me, I'll show you what will really put me to sleep,"

The man stated, "Those straps stay on, Bosses orders,"

"Okay, then you will never put me to sleep, and you'll never know the intense pleasure of making love to a Mandroid."

The man walked to the gurney, saying, "I'm Isador, "He freed Patsy. She sat on the right side of the stretcher and held the sheet close to her chest with her left arm as Isador put his arms around her. But before he could do anything. Patsy grabbed his energy pistol strapped to his side and stunned him. Dropped the bed sheet, stepped over an unconscious Isador, and dressed.

General Lars and the doctor entered the room, and the General shouted, "What are you doing free?"

Patsy flipped the gurney on its side, crouched behind it, and fired, stunning them both. She made her way to the control room, barged in, and ordered the woman at the controls, "Step away from the computer consul," Patsy then fired a long blast of energy at the massive computer destroying it.

The woman asked, "What did you do that for? The General needed it to look for his lost daughter."

"No, the General was using it to drag me here so he could rip me open and steal the key inside me,"

"I'm Cathy Loganberry. So, you're the one Lars has been talking about. I know how to get you out of here, but you are gonna have to give me your gun."

"So, you can turn me over to Lars, not on your life."

Cathy stated, "There are a dozen guards between here and the outside door, and every one of them can fry you to a crisp before you can put your finger on the gun,"

A reluctant Patsy handed Cathy her energy pistol. She quickly spun her around, shoved the pistol in her side, saying, "Now will do things my way,"

Just then, two guards rushed in brandishing energy pistols shouting, "Freeze!"

Cathy stated with a smile, "I'm taking the prisoner to the lady's room. Now if you don't want to clean up a mess, I'd move,"

In the lady's room with its white, porcelain walls and stainless-steel sink Cathy took a light blue three-inch in diameter compact from her purse, opened it, and pressed a red button. A two-dimensional eight feet in diameter oval appeared. Kathy stated, "It's time for action, so step through it before the general charges in,"

Patsy questions, "Who are you?"

"I'm the one who has been setting you free every time the General dragged you in here. Your memory loss was because Lars used a mind probe to get information out of that head of yours; now let's go,"

The women tumbled through the portal and fell against a tall Pine tree. Cathy helped Patsy to her feet, saying, "Dang,"

"What's wrong," inquired Patsy.

"The portal was supposed to open in Moon Base One, not here in the Beaverhead Deer Lodge National Forest."

"And pray tell, where is that?" asked Patsy.

"Somewhere in the lower southwest corner of Montana. If my memory serves me correctly, Lake Browns should be north of here,"

Patsy asked, "What is it that you are not telling me,"

"I think General Lars has one of his war cruiser hidden somewhere close to earth,"

"Wouldn't Moon Base One pick it up on their scanner,"

"Not if he had it cloaked just above the planet,"

On the east end of Browns Lake, Patsy pointed to two men on the beach and said, "Maybe they'll give us something to eat,"

The women entered the campsite; Cathy admired the two red dirt bikes and asked, "Would you kind gentlemen have a morsel of food for two starving ladies?"

A short man in his thirties with a beard clad in black leather handed the women a bowl of beans and hotdogs, saying, "I'm Darrell, and that is my friend Jose. What brings you lovely ladies here in the middle of nowhere,"

Patsy stated, "We are lost and haven't a clue as to where we are going."

Jose asked, "Have you been able to contact someone for help,"

Patsy chuckled, saying, "How are we going to do that when there is no signal for our iPhones,"

Darrell stated, "It's gonna be dark in a couple of hours; what say you and your friend camp here for the night,"

Cathy stated, "Thank you but no thanks,"

Darrell stated, "Seeing you are in the middle of this forest close to nightfall, you don't have a choice, so pick a tent, and we'll join you."

Cathy took her pink and yellow energy pistol out of her purse and pointed at the men saying, "Get on your bikes and leave before I vaporize you where you stand,"

Darrell laughed and said, "Look, Jose, the lady has a toy ray gun, and she's gonna shoot us,"

Cathy vaporized a nearby boulder saying, "This is no toy, so move it," then fired a blast of energy that struck the sand inches from Darrell's feet,"

With the men gone, Patsy helped herself to another bowl of beans, sat on a nearby log, and asked, "Where to from here,"

"I haven't a clue. But I sent the distress signal on my computer watch, which means Prayerfully, we'll be rescued before Darrell and his friend returns. That means one of us stands guard while the other sleep,"

Patsy stated, "I'm not worried because I don't think they will be coming back,"

"Trust me when I say, If we don't have a guard, we will wake in the morning with them snuggled up to us,"

As the sun was just above the horizon, Cathy fell asleep but was startled when Darrell yanked the energy pistol out of her hand. Jose dragged Patsy out of her tent by her feet with her screaming, "You touch me, and you are gonna be in big trouble."

Darrell and Jose stood with their backs to the forest, and Jose asked, "Which one do you want,"

Cathy smiled, saying, "No nookie for you guys because you are about to get the pounding of your life,"

Jose laughed, saying, "Who's going to do it? You?"

Cathy stated, "No, him,"

Just then, two massive hands grabbed Darrell and Jose's shoulders. They turned around and saw a ten-foot-tall giant clad in jeans and a green plaid shirt. The giant stated in a deep voice, "No hurt little Misses' friends or Edhu crush,"

Sprite Pixy, dressed in a burgundy slack suit, waved from Edhu's right shoulder, saying, "Hi guys, Calistus picked up your distress signal and sent me to help,"

Pixy flew down and said, "Hey Patsy, I haven't seen you in a coon's age. What have you been up to?" Pixy held up her index finger, saying, "Hold that thought for a moment," she turned to Darrel and Jose, saying, "I'll give you guys just five minutes to pack up your trash and get out of here, or I'll have my little friend sig his big brother on you,"

After Jose and Darrel bid a hasty retreat, Pixy asked, "So Patsy, where have you been all these months?"

Patsy hung her head, saying, "I wish I knew. Terrie told me that she found me while she was digging around some old ruins. But all I can remember is waking up on a park bench with a gold scrolled key in my purse with everybody and their brother after me,"

Cathy reported, "General Lars has a war cruiser hidden somewhere close to earth and has one of his cronies posing as Jeff to locate the key for him,"

"Where is the key now," asked Pixy.

"Inside Patsy, along with the alien computer," stated Cathy.

A frustrated Patsy hollered, "You guys knew about the key all along and didn't tell me? I married that slimy thing, Jeff, and got into it with him for crying out loud!"

Pixy said goodbye to Edhu and said, "Patrick and Alexis should be here in about a half hour, and those two guys, Darrel and Jose, were Slime heads."

"They were what? And you let them go," shouted an enraged Patsy.

Just then, Jose and Darrel calmly strolled up to Patsy, and Darrel said, "I'll cut to the chase. Give us the two halves of the key, and we'll be gone,"

Patsy clinched her fist by her side in silent anger, with thoughts of how she was abused by the General. She let go of a scream and stretched her arms towards the men. A blast of white energy shot out of her fists, vaporizing Darrel, and Jose. Patsy then staggered sideways, trying to maintain her balance. Cathy caught her saying, "I've got you, girl," Sat Patsy on the ground then said to Pixy, "Tell Thor, The Galaxy Sentinel, why the General is after the key,"

Patsy walked away from the group in anger, wondering why they were treating her as the enemy. Some distance away, she sat on the ground and leaned back against a fur tree and thought about the trouble the key had caused her. Patsy stood, circled to the south shore of the lake, placed her hand on her stomach, and said, "Computer power down," she suddenly felt weak and collapsed on the ground, unable to move. Then she thought, "Oh crap, what have I done," She tried to turn on the alien computer inside her, but nothing she said worked.

As the days slowly passed, Patsy lay on the ground and thought about all the dumb things she did in her life. Just then, a fifteen-hundred-pound brown bear sauntered up to her and began to sniff her legs. A terrified Patsy lay perfectly still, praying the bear wouldn't tear her apart. She then heard a man question, "What'ch find Brownie."

A man in his forties, clad in jeans, ragged blue shirt, and a long scraggly dark brown beard approached her with his mule. I Knelt and felt Patsy's neck to see if she was alive.

Patsy whimpered, "I can't move."

The man put Patsy on his mule and brought her to his log cabin, where he bathed and fed her every day for two weeks.

One day as the man was washing Patsy, she sat up in bed and said, "Thank you, I don't know what I would have done if you didn't happen by."

The man smiled and said, "They call me The Prospector, and you would have died from exposure. From the tone of your voice and the texture of your skin, I'd say you are some kind of a fancy robot,"

Patsy gave out a sigh of relief and then stated, "I am what's called a Mandroid; all the organs in my body are artificial. However, because of a horse-riding accident, they put my brain in the skull of this mechanical contrivance. I can eat, sleep, and do all the normal things of any woman except have kids. But some two weeks ago I did something foolish which caused me to be incapacitated. Thanks for the sponge bath but prayerfully, within time, I will regain my strength. When I do, would you mind assisting me with my shower activities and things? I can pay you,"

The Prospector thought for a moment, then said, "As long as you wear your underwear bottoms, I'll help you, and don't worry about paying me; friends help friends in time of need,"

Some days later, The Prospector was in the living room writing something in a book. Patsy limped up the hall in her powder blue step-ins and said, "I'm gonna take my shower now,"

The Prospector stopped what he was doing and stared at Patsy with a smile on his face and talked to her for almost twenty minutes, secretly enjoying her shapely figure.

Because of all the abuse that came her way, since she had the key, she was starved for attention and enjoyed the Prospector talking to her before her shower. But the Prospector refused to help Patsy in the shower or wash her back because he felt it was wrong. As the weeks slowly passed, Patsy became comfortable around the Prospector and didn't wear anything when she casually strolled up the hall to tell him she was going to shower, wanting his attention. But, when the Prospector took Patsy out for a bite, he kept his distance because he was concerned she would look to him as more than a friend.

One day Patsy had finished her shower, dried off, didn't bother to put her clothes on, and walked into the kitchen for a glass of water. The

Prospector walked in and snapped, "I don't want to see you like that, so put your clothes on!"

Patsy dressed, made a pot of coffee, then sat outside with a mug.

The Prospector sat on her right and took a swallow of his coffee. Patsy stated, "I thank you for my sponge baths when I couldn't move and allowed me to limp to the bathroom without worrying how I was dressed. I also loved the attention you gave me when we talked just before I stepped in the shower. But you didn't have to silently struggle with your sexual desires when I showered. Because we could have prayed about your situation. I know you wanted to get into it with me because you accidentally, on purpose, let me see things I shouldn't have,"

The Prospector stated in mock innocence, "I have no idea what you are talking about,"

"Yeah, you do, but you don't want to admit it."

"I maintained modesty around you at all times, and you know it."

"Did you forget about the time you walked in the kitchen in the buff, looked at me, then told me that you thought I was outside when you knew right where I was? Then there were all those times you dressed, with your bedroom door open and knew I could see what you were doing because my bedroom is across from yours. What about all those times you dried my back after my shower because my right arm wouldn't work. You're a man living alone, living for the Lord, then you find me, and your sexual desires are aroused. You then became concerned about being pure before your Saviour, so you left me to struggle on my own. When we went out for a walk, all you had to do was let me put my hand on your shoulder so I could steady myself. But you were too busy trying to be righteous and keeping an emotional distance from me; you turned your back on someone in need. Because of your actions, you remind me of the pharisee in the story of the Good Samaritan,"

The Prospector stated, "You have me confused with someone else because I never dried your back at any time, and I never let you see me naked. As far as my bedroom door being open when I dress and undress, It is closed at all times."

"I am sorry that I made you feel uncomfortable when I showered, but I believe that it was alright for you to see me without anything on because I had a need, and the Bible says to help those in need. But you are a great friend, and I could not have made it without your help," Patsy looked at the Prospector and said, "Could you stand and face me,"

The Prospector put his mug of coffee down, stood, and asked, "Now what,"

Patsy promptly stood, threw her arms around him, gave him a long boob-crushing hug, then kissed his lips. Stepped back and said, "feel better? That's probably the first hug and kiss you've had in years. Go in your bedroom, take off your shirt, and lay on the bed so I can give you a back rub,"

13

Clearing the air

Patsy said goodbye to the Prospector, made her way east through the wooded mountains to Rout I-15, then south to Dillon, Montana, and stayed in Motel 6, thankful to be away from the Prospector, and grabbed some much-needed sleep. Then went to the Blacktail Station Stake house for a late lunch. She loved the white linen tablecloths covered with glass and ordered the biggest stake they had on the menu. After gorging herself, Patsy walked to Jaycee park on East Sebree Street, sat on the lush green grass, and watched a young couple play tennis. When the couple had finished their game, Patsy heard a man say, "There you are. Do you know how long it took to find you,"

Patsy moaned softly and thought, *"Patrick is not going to be standing right behind me when I turn around. Better yet, I'm gonna ignore whoever it is, and maybe they'll go away,"*

Patrick stood in front of Patsy and inquired, "Why did you take off like that? Tom or one of his cronies could have found you,"

Patsy stood to her feet, grabbed Patrick by his shirt, picked him up, saying, "I am tired of all your lies and treating me like a no nothing. You little man are going to have your first flying lesson," and went to throw Patrick as far as she could.

Softy quietly approached Patsy's left side and slapped just below her left shoulder. Patsy suddenly dropped to the ground with Patrick on top of her.

Alexus stated, "We need to get her back to our place ASAP,"

In a country bungalow on Legget Avenue, Alexis laid an unconscious Patsy on the bed in the spare bedroom, then turned her back on.

Patsy opened her eyes and asked, "Patrick, are you going to tell me another string of lies?"

Alexis stated, "No one lied to you about the key, and who's been after you. We were aware of the key and what it could possibly do, and the General is power hungry, but that's all."

Gideon Bear waddled in, tapped Alexis' left leg, and looked up at her. Alexis picked up the bear and put him on the bed. Gideon looked at Patsy's face, then lay down and nuzzled her.

With tears in her eyes, Patsy held Gideon in her arms, saying, "If Gideon says it's alright, then it's alright with me. How did you find me when I turned off that fancy computer in me?"

Patrick answered, "The power source will still give off a signal that I could track. But for the last month, there was no signal,"

"When I shut down the alien computer, I fell to the ground, unable to move. A few days later, The Prospector happened by, took me to his place, and nursed me back to health,"

Alexis said, "You mean Mike Johnson took care of you for the month you were missing? Didn't you say that the Lord told you two were incompatible?"

Patsy sat up, stared at Alexis, and said, "That name sounds familiar,"

Alexis stated, "It should; you only dated him for over a year and wound up stressed out and frustrated."

"Did I ever complain to you about Mike?" questioned Patsy.

"More times than I can count, about how he would ignore you when you went out to dinner, and how he would push you away when you responded to the sweet way he spoke to you,"

Patrick asked, "What do you know about General Lars,"

Patsy got out of bed, saying, "He has a war cruiser hidden just above this planet and has a laboratory somewhere on this continent and has been bringing me there to get the key, but Cathy kept smuggling me out of there. The reason why I have a memory loss is Lars did a mind probe on me, which wiped out my memory."

Patrick stated, "Mind probes were banned in the Alliance for that reason."

Alice rushed into the bedroom and gave Patsy a hug saying, "I've been doing a lot of praying for your safety. You're gonna have to tell me all about your secret rendezvous with a guy, and don't you dare leave out any of the spicy stuff,"

Patsy stated, "I almost forgot, before I escaped from General Lars, I destroyed his computer so he can't locate me or transport me to his lab ever again,"

Alice reported, "Patrick, I was talking to Susie J. Parkers, I mean, Terrie J. Parkers, the other day and gave her a bunch of false information about us. She still goes by Susie J. Parkers to hide that she is Terrie, who works for Tom. Anyway, She told me that she didn't find Patsy while digging around some old ruins. A scientist who shall remain nameless stole Terrie's diamond studded purse with the key and gave it to Patsy at her engagement party with Mike Jonson. Patsy was to deliver the key to the Galaxy Sentinel. But Terrie told Tom what happened, and Tom reported it to General Lars. He located Patsy and the key, transported her to his lab, and did a mind probe on her, which wiped out Patsy's memory. That's why she came too on that park bench with Susie Parker's purse. The Galaxy Sentinel was one step ahead of the General and had planted Cathy there, who helped Patsy escape, and the General has been trying to get the key back ever since,"

Patsy stated loudly, "Come on, Alice, it's time we went for coffee,"

"I know just the place, BB café, and Boutique; I'll drive. Because I don't want you disappearing on me while you're behind the wheel,"

At the café forty-five minutes later, Patsy ordered a large coffee, ham, egg, and cheese on an English muffin, while Alice ordered a medium coffee and a Sour Dough Bread Sandwich and sat in a booth with Patsy. She took a swallow of her coffee and said, "Tell me about the secret rendezvous you had with Mike,"

"There was no secret meeting with Mike. I stormed off, steaming mad, and turned off my computer. What I didn't know was that it was powering my systems, so I lay on the ground, unable to move for three days. The Prospector found me, brought me to his place, and gave me a sponge bath until I could function on my own. When I regained my strength, I said goodbye and left. I did not have any nooky with the Prospector, and I definitely did not sleep with him, although it did cross my mind about sneaking into his bedroom late at night. But I kept falling asleep before I could, and he was up early in the morning to make breakfast.

Alice asked, "Is your memory coming back?"

Patsy stated, "More than that, It's back. I wanna see Jeff ASAP,"

A reluctant Alice said, "Alright I'll make the arrangements, but watch yourself around him,"

Later the next day, Patsy, dressed in her short red dress with the V neckline, made her way down Deerfield Lane, then headed east to Beaverhead River. She took off her shoes and socks, then sat on the bank with her feet in the water, waiting for Jeff to come along and act the way Mike did when she would sit on the riverbank.

Some thirteen minutes later, Jeff approached Patsy behind her and massaged her shoulders.

Patsy inquired, "Is that all you're gonna do?"

"I can't rub your feet when they are in the water,"

Patsy lay on her stomach with her left hand in the water, saying, "It's been a hot one today,"

Jeff lay by Patsy's side, softly stroking the back of her legs, slowly working his way up to her thigh.

When Jeff was about to lift Patsy's dress, she said, "So Mike, what have you been doing since I disappeared during our engagement announcement party? Or should I call you the Prospector," Patsy sat up, saying, "You are a man of many personalities, but I forgive you. Now take off your shirt so that I can see that fabulous chest of yours,"

Jeff asked, "Why are you calling me Mike? I'm Jeff. Has your memory slipped that much?"

Patsy stated, "When I would sit on the riverbank and dangle my feet in the water, I would say certain phrases to let Mike know what I wanted him to do to me next. You responded perfectly to every phrase, so you, my dear man, are Mike and the Prospector,"

Jeff took his shirt off, saying, "You got me; I was Mike and the Prospector because I was trying to jog your memory. Forgive me,"

Once Jeff had his shirt off, Patsy gently rubbed his muscles, took a pocketknife out of her purse, and slashed his chest, then said, "How about that, you're not even a Mandroid. Because if you were, you would not bleed, Because the heart pumps the blood directly to the brain to keep it alive, and the body is mechanical. Who are you? Because the real Jeff showed up a week ago,"

"I'M a Lazartran. That's all you need to know,"

Patsy took an energy pistol from her purse, pointed it at Jeff, and asked, "Did General Lars hire you to keep tabs on me?"

Jeff stated, "After you escaped from the General's lab, he traced you to that park bench and set it up so we would meet in the forest. You were so desperate for a man it was easy to get you to marry me, and that cream I put on your back was supposed to make your mind putty in my hands. Then Patrick came along and spoiled everything,"

Jeff swiftly batted the energy pistol out of Patsy's hand, picked it up, saying, "I Hate to kill you, but the General wants what's inside you,"

Before Jeff could pull the trigger, A gun was shoved in his back, and Softy stated, "Drop the gun, or I'll waste you right where you stand,"

Patsy took the energy pistol away from Jeff and said, "Meet my twin, Softy," She picked up a red CO2 fire extinguisher from behind the bush and then blasted Jeff with it.

Jeff's eyes rolled back in his head as he collapsed to the ground unconscious and Patsy smiled and said, "Yep, he's a cold-blooded Lazartran, alright,"

Softy and Patsy put Jeff in the cold river to keep his body temperature down until someone from the Galaxy Sentinel took him away.

In a nearby coffee shop, Patsy ordered two large coffees for them and sat in a booth. Patsy took a swallow of her coffee and then said, "Softy, I have to pick that computerized brain of yours. Miss Parkers says that she found me and the key while she was digging in some ruins. However, Alice says that the key was given to me by a professor after he stole it from her. I remember being at Susie's dig, but Gideon and I were trying to escape a gang of thugs who were after us,"

Softy stated, "It is well known that Susie Joan Parker can't tell the truth to save her life. It's possible those thugs overpowered you, then buried you and Gideon to hide the evidence. Susie came along later and found you and was about to kill you and turn the key over to the General. But he transported Patsy to his lab before she could,"

"That sounds like what happened. Thank you. Now if you will excuse me, I have to use the lady's room."

When Patsy returned, Softy was gone and raced outside, saw her being forced into the back of a van by four men in jeans, and shouted, "Leave her alone!"

The four men stared at Patsy, then at Softy, and one shouted, "We nabbed the wrong one! Get her!"

As soon as they let Softy go, she ripped off the sliding door on the side of the van and hit the men with it sending them sprawling on the parking lot, and the driver of the van sped away.

When the four men revived, Softy glared at them, saying, "Tell General Lars that Softy Mullins is coming to take him out," She picked up the van door and threw it skyward.

With their mouths open in shock, the men stared at the door until it disappeared in the clouds, then rushed off.

Patsy high-fived Softy saying, "Don't mess with the Mullens Sisters. I just wish you would have been around when the Garden Romeo forced himself on me,"

"You have the key so you can take me back in time so that I can kick his royal butt,"

"I can't because I turned it off,"

Softy stated, "No problem," touched Patsy's stomach, then said, "It's on,"

"Are you sure? I don't feel any different,"

"That's because when the Professor put the alien computer inside you, It immediately accessed your body's systems to power them. When you turned the alien computer off, the miniature subatomic generator that was designed to power your systems kicked in, and it took time for you to regain your strength,"

Patsy took Softy into the lady's room, touched her shoulder, saying, "Key, bring us back to Odessa nine hundred and ninety-eight years ago,"

Patsy glanced around, saying, "I guess it didn't work this time because we're still in the Lady's room."

Softy stated with a smile, "Wait for it,"

Patsy said, "Nothing is happening," opened the restroom door, and entered the Garden of Odessa.

Softy slowly scanned the exotic flowers forcing her attention on a deep blue eight-inch-in diameter rose, and said, "That is one huge flower. Now, where is Horas?"

Patsy showed Softy the deep red Fire Bushed of HP5, the pink Creeping Vines of Avalon Prime, and the Whispering Falls of the Blue Ringed System. She then pointed to a group of eight feet high orange bushes saying, "Horace should be behind them making out with someone. I can't help you because, right now, I am in a hospital, unable to walk."

Softy slowly walked around the huge bushes and saw a tall man in his early twenties with curly brown hair heavily involved kissing a young woman in her late twenties with black hair down to her hips. As Horace was taking off the woman's blouse, Softy stated loudly, "Up to your same old tricks, seducing innocent young girls,"

Horace stared at Softy and said, "Patsy, you're out of the hospital so soon. I, I was going to see you tomorrow,"

"I am not Patsy, I'm her twin sister Softy Mulleins, and it's payback time,"

The young girl held her blouse to her chest and stated, "It wasn't Horace's fault that woman was knocked off her hoarse by that tree,"

Softy said, "Didn't Romeo tell you that the day before Patsy's accident, Horace raped her on this very spot which caused serious emotional problems and is the reason she is in the medical center."

The woman stared at Horace in shock, then said, "You Pig," put on her top, and left.

Softy lifted Horace by his shirt, stood him on his feet, brushed the dirt off his clothes, then kicked him between his pockets, sending him down on his knees, groaning in pain.

Horace stood, saying, "I usually don't hit women, but, in your case, I'll make an exception and kicked Softy in her stomach. Softy shook off the blow and landed a hard right cross to his jaw, knocking him out.

A minute later, a Garden security approached, glanced at Horace, then said, "I see the Garden Romeo met his match,"

14

Patsy Corrects Softy

Patsy and Softy caught up to the young woman who was heavily involved in kissing Horace. Patsy ducked behind a rose bush as Softy touched the woman's right shoulder and asked, "Are you alright?"

"I will be in a while. I'm Jackie and thank you for coming along when you did because that Pig was forcing me into something I didn't want to do. Now the problem is to say no to that Pig the next time he asks me for a date,"

"Horace most likely puts some kind of a love potion on his lips, so the woman he kisses will do whatever he wants but don't worry, he was arrested on multiple assault charges."

"Then poor Patsy wasn't the only one he fooled around with,"

"You've heard of the Garden Romeo,"

"Who hasn't, but no one knows who he is,"

"The one you were getting it on with was the Garden Romeo,"

A stunned Jackie stared at Softy silently, shocked that she was almost Romeo's next victim.

After Jackie left, Softy studied Patsy's countenance and asked, "What's wrong?"

"I was thinking I could send you back to our time, then hop a space cruiser to some distant planet and live the rest of my life in peace."

"That alien computer inside you will attract attention no matter where you go, and you know it,"

In a split-second, Softy appeared in the women's room but not Patsy.

Softy shook her head and moaned, "When will Patsy ever learn to listen to other people's advice,"

Just then, a wet nude Patsy appeared shouting, "Yes! I'm back."

Softy asked, "Where are your clothes,"

"I was swimming and ran into trouble with a guy and had to do some quick thinking, and here I am. Oh, by the way, Softy, in the Odessa era, which was the year 1025, The traditional culture was to swim either naked or in your underwear. So, I swam sans clothes, and the rest is history."

"In other words, you don't want to talk about it."

"You got it sis,"

Patsy stated, "Key, give me a complete change of clothes,"

In seconds, a woman's clothes for a five-year-old a thousand years ago appeared on the sink. Patsy muttered, "Dang," She then stated, "Key, give me a pair of powder blue undies with a matching brassiere, a pair of blue jeans, socks and sneakers, and a blue blouse that will fit me, oh and a bath towel,"

A second later, Patsy stared at the clothes on the counter, picked up a pair of pantaloons and a corset, and asked, "What, pray tell are these?"

Softy stated, "Remember, it's an alien computer and has no idea what women factions are in today's society,"

"At least I can wear the extra-long panties and slacks and the top."

Once Patsy was dressed, Softy stated, "You and I have to talk, but this time I'll buy the coffee."

Sitting in a booth away from everyone, Softy took a swallow of her latte and said, "You are your own worst enemy."

A puzzled Patsy asked, "Can you expound on that if you please,"

Softy asked, "You are running down a narrow path and are distracted by something. What would happen?"

"I'd smack into a tree because I wasn't looking where I was going,"

"Exactly. You, Patsy, have taken your eyes off the Lord and allowed men to distract you,"

"Why would you say something like that about me?" questioned a puzzled Patsy.

"Ever since you became a Mandroid, you've been rejected and abused by everyone. The wound Horace gave you when he forced himself on you started you fighting for attention emotionally. When you worked for Thor at the Institute, you did everything possible to gain people's attention. But you weren't satisfied, so you moved to Earth and hooked up with Mike because he paid attention to you, and you forgot what the Word of God said about relationships. When Jeff came along, he knew how to pull your strings and got you to marry him and jeopardized your responsibility to protect the key. By the time the Prospector came into your life, you were so starved for attention you flaunted your nude body at him and let him do whatever he wanted, and don't tell me you didn't because I know you did. I'll end with this: the only reason you are not pregnant by the Prospector is you are a Mandroid."

Patsy stated, "Before you go any further with your string of derogatory comments about my private life. Mike and the Prospector were Jeff, so messing around with the Prospector, I was with my husband. I know this because the Prospector's mannerisms were identical to Jeff and Mike."

A shocked Softy asked, "You knew this and didn't tell anyone,"

"I discovered who the Prospector was when he gave me my first sponge bath, but I didn't let on that I knew who he was. Plus, the three of them have the same scar on the lower part of their back."

Softy stated, "But your marriage to Jeff was null and void because he didn't get a blood test."

"I did some investigation into my marriage to Jeff, and according to the law of the Planetary Alliance, I am still married to him. I didn't say anything because everyone thinks Jeff, Mike, and the Prospector are three different people. But what do you know, you're a robot.

Softy stated, "I'm more of a robot than you realize, but I won't bore you with the details."

Alice rushed in, all out of breath, saying, "They just dismissed Jeff because there was not enough evidence to hold him. Which means he's out and is going to kill the both of you."

Patsy handed Alice ten dollars, saying, "Treat yourself and join us."

An excited Alice hollered, "Didn't you guys hear me? Jeff is gunning for you two, which means you're dead. So, get out of here before he gets here,"

Softy stated, "Patsy said, sit!"

About thirty-three minutes later, Jeff stormed into the coffee shop, hollering, "Softy and Patsy, you two are dead meat for tricking me into being arrested. Now you two die!"

The coffee shop quickly emptied when Jeff pointed his energy pistol at the women.

Alice looked up, saying, "Lord Jesus, I'm coming home," she closed her eyes and waited for death.

Patsy placed her hands on her friend's backs, saying, "We're good," as an energy field around the women glowed a bright yellow when a blast from Jeff's gun hit it.

Patsy then rose to her feet and glared at Jeff, saying, "It's been said a Lazratren can take a lot of punishment. Do you mind if I try that myth out on you?"

Patsy grabbed Jeff by his shoulders and fell backward, throwing him over her and against the far wall. Before Jeff could stand, Patsy took hold of one foot and hand, spun around, and sent him flying across the coffee shop. She then hammered his face with her fist for a good minute. Patsy picked Jeff up by his shoulders and said, "That beating was for tricking me into marrying you. This is for trying to kill my friends and me." And hit him between his pockets, sending him to his knees, moaning in pain.

Jeff stated, "You can't kill an unarmed man; it's murder." He saw the fierce look in Patsy's eyes and nervously said, "Please don't do this to me; no, don't!" Jeff let go an agonizing scream, then quickly stopped when his body exploded into dust."

Alice stared at Patsy in horror and asked, "What did you do that for,"

Patsy stated, "The Alliance and Odessa support the avenger of blood, which is me."

"But Jeff didn't kill anyone." Stated Alice.

Jeff tried to kill me dozens of times, and if it weren't for the energy barrier the key put around us, we would be micro dust right now."

Terrie ran up to Patsy and asked, "What did you do to my Jeff."

Patsy, Softy, and Alice escorted Terrie to the country bungalow on Legget Avenue. Turned her off, put her in a spare bedroom, and removed both legs so she wouldn't take off on them. When Terrie opened her eyes, clad in a yellow nightgown, she hollered, "Where are my legs,"

Patrick entered the bedroom with her limbs and stated, "We can't let you go because of your involvement with Tom and Jeff."

"What are you talking about? You sent me there to spy on them; now you accuse me of siding with those traitors."

"I have proof that the three of you plotted to kill Patsy for the key. Now tell me why you are working for General Lars when you knew he would use the power of the key to destroy the Alliance and every peace-loving planet in the galaxy."

"First, tell me why you murdered Jeff," screamed Terrie.

Patrick stated, "The real Jeff is being held on Moon Base One. What you were infatuated with was a Lazertran disguised as Jeff."

Terrie gagged then said, "You mean, I did you know what, with a Slime Head that's gross and disgusting, I would never do that because I know the difference."

Alexis chased her husband out, closed the bedroom door, lubricated the joints of her limbs, then put them on and said, "You most likely have to freshen up. Then I want to talk to you about something important."

Some fifteen minutes later, Terrie sat on the right side of the bed, took a swallow of her coffee, and asked, "What is it that you wanted to talk to me about,"

"How is your walk with Christ?"

"Good; why do you ask,"

"Because your lewd actions with Jeff tell me otherwise."

Terry hung her head, saying, "It's not something I am proud of. All we wanted to do was get the key from Patsy without hurting her. But somewhere along the line, Tom turned mean and nasty, and no, he is not a Slime Head, that much I know. Jeff was to trick Patsy into marrying him and get the key; then, we were to head for parts unknown. Then Tom wanted to kill Patsy, and I became emotionally entangled with Jeff, and my walk with Christ went sour,"

"You two still got into it even though Jeff was married to Patsy,"

"Yes, Jeff told me that the marriage to Patsy was a fake, and he never slept with her."

Alexis stated, "According to the Alliance, Jeff was married to Patsy and was a husband to Patsy in every sense of the word."

Terrie stated, "I still can't believe I horsed around with a Slime Head and didn't know it."

Alexis asked, "Did you notice the scar on the lower part of his back?"

"Yes, I have, and I asked Jeff when it happened, but he wouldn't tell me."

'Alexis smiled then stated, "Because a Mandroids skin is artificial, they don't scar,"

Terrie muttered, "Oh crap, you're right,"

Just then, the real Jeff entered the bedroom, gave Terrie a hug, then said, "Hi, Love Muffin. Why are you still in your nighty this late in the day,"

Terrie stated, "Take off your shirt and lower your pants,"

"In front of her," pointing to Alexis.

Alexis turned her back as Jeff removed his shirt and pants and asked, "Are you sure you want to fool around with her in the room,"

Terrie inched Jeff's BVDs down a bit, then said with a smile, "Good, you don't have a scar on the lower part of their back,"

A baffled Jeff asked, "What are you talking about? Mandroids don't scar,"

Alexis turned back around, stared at Jeff, and said, "Don't go anywhere," she then left and returned with a knife and a dozen small bottles and said, "I have to get some samples, so take off your underwear,"

A half-hour later, Alexis put the small bottles in a box, turned to leave, and heard Terrie say to Jeff, "Put your clothes on because we are not going to fool around until after we are married,"

After dinner on the back patio, Patrick said to Jeff, "I tested the samples my wife gave me, and you are all Mandroid. Now can you tell me when you were abducted,"

Terrie clung to Jeff's right arm as he stated, "It was shortly after Patsy came to Earth. A scientist wanted me to introduce him to Patsy because he wanted her to do something for her, and it was very important. That evening I invited Patsy to dinner and introduced him to Patsy, and after dinner, I was abducted,"

Patrick asked, "Did you know General Lars wants the key and is using Tom to get it for him."

"I don't know how to capture the General, but I can give you Tom, just don't ask me to be a mole,"

15

Doubleganger Returns

Two days later, the front doorbell rang, Terrie opened it and said, "Alexis, I thought you were in the shower. What did you do, climb out the bathroom window?"

"I'm not Alexis; I'm Doubleganger; remember, you left me in the closet."

"You're slipping on your jokes, Alexis because this one is very poor,"

Just then, Alexis approached Terrie with a deep blue bath towel wrapped around her and said, "Doubleganger, you're alive! How did you find us?"

"It wasn't easy,"

Terrie did a double take, then said, "Patsy, pour me a mug of strong black coffee."

Patrick walked up to Doubleganger, gave her a passionate kiss saying, "You look ravishing today, me Firefly,"

Alexis shouted, "Bug-a-Boo, take your hands off Doubleganger, now!"

Patrick spun around with his eyes open wide, saying, "Hi me, Firefly, nice towel."

Alexis took Doubleganger by her hand, saying, "Lady, you need a makeover because the last thing I want is you in bed with my Bub-a-Boo,"

"But I like the way I look." stated a confused Doubleganger.

Hours later, Alexis brought Doubleganger to the supper table with Blond hair, no glasses, clad in white hot pants and a modest long sleeve pink blouse, and asked, "What do you guys think? Oh, her new name is D-G,"

Softy asked, "How did you remove her freckles?"

"I discovered the chemical composition of hydrogen peroxide would easily remove the freckles from D-G's artificial skin,"

While everyone was enjoying their apple pie and ice cream after supper. Tom boldly walked in, greeted everyone, Then locked his gaze on Jeff and said, "I thought Patsy vaporized you,"

Jeff stated, "You know what they say, you can't keep a good man down,"

Tom growled, "Terrie, Jeff, I wanna speak to you two outside,"

Outside on the front porch, Tom questioned, "What's the big idea of siding with the enemy? You two were given orders from the General to Kill Patsy and get the alien computer and key,"

Terrie stated, "News flash, Tom, Patsy is protected by the key; meaning anyone who tries to get it will wind up dead, and I, for one, want to live for a very long time,"

Tom stared at Jeff, saying, "You're her husband When you are in bed with her. Get her emotionally excited; that will temporarily disable the key's defensive system and will give you time to put a knife through her heart and get the key. When you have it, contact me at this address,"

That night, Jeff rolled over in bed, kissed Patsy then said, "I can't do it,"

"Can't do what?" questioned Patsy.

"Tom said that if I get you excited, that will disable the key's defensive system and will give me time to kill you to get it, but I will not murder the one I love."

Patsy stated, "There's only one solution to this, and that is to give Tom what he wants,"

The next day Patsy knocked on the door to Tom's place, then entered saying, "You want the Key, you can have it,"

"It's not that easy; the key will protect you if I try and take it,"

"Is there a way to temporarily disable the key?"

Tom smiled and said, "If I get you sexually excited, that will disable its defenses long enough for me to get the key,"

Patsy stated, "I lived long enough. Get me sexually excited so you can kill me for the key,"

Tom stated, "The bedroom awaits,"

On the way to the bedroom, Patsy took off her top, saying, "How about a kiss stud muffin,"

As Tom put his arms around Patsy, she said, "First, I should shed these clothes," Patsy reached inside her Bra, took out a long thin knife, and smiled, saying, "How did that get in there? So don't worry, I won't hurt you. Now, how about that kiss,"

Tom wrapped his arms around Patsy, then staggered backward, staring at the knife in his chest.

Patsy apologized, then said, "I am so sorry; I didn't mean to do that. Here let me help you." Patsy shoved the knife up to the hilt, saying, "Time to die, evil man,"

A short time later, she stared at a dead Tom lying on the hall floor, took his energy pistol from the nightstand, and vaporized his body and everything that would say he was from another planet. She took the communicator from under his mattress and called the General.

Lars answered saying, "I told you not to contact me this time of the day, and why are you silent,"

Patsy gripped the communicator tightly, saying, "I killed Tom, and I'm coming after you," Patsy then vaporized the communicator,

Sitting alone in a coffee shop, Patsy placed her hands around her mug of coffee, saying softly, "Lord, You are wonderful, and it is because of the finished work on the Cross I stand in your thrown room rejoicing because of the victory in my life. Can you forgive me for killing Tom Marks? I couldn't think of any other way to end all his evil, murderess harassment against me."

D-G sat next to Patsy with a mug of strawberry tea and asked, "Am I too late to stop you from killing Tom?"

A sorrowful Patsy stated, "Yes. By the way, how did you find me because? I told no one where I was going,"

D-G took a swallow of her tea and then said, "I was made from an alien computer and have the ability to track Mandroids,"

Patsy looked at D-G, saying, "You were going to go after Tom because you thought Alexis was in danger,"

"Softy and I are clones, and as clones, we protect the one we were cloned from."

Softy entered the coffee shop, sat on Patsy's right, took a swallow of her latte, then said, "You contacted the General, didn't you."

"Yeah, right after I killed Tom. Why,"

"That was foolish and a dumb thing to do, especially when he's out to kill you,"

Patsy glanced at the one-foot square package on Softy's lap and asked, "What's in the pretty box,"

"Just a little something for the General that he will get a blast out of,"

Just then, General Lars entered the coffee shop clad in earth-style military garb. Approached Softy saying, "Give me the Key, or I will destroy this place with you and your friends in it,"

Softy held tightly onto the box on her lap, saying, "You can't have it,"

The General wrenched the box out of Softy's hands, then said, "It's in here, isn't it,"

"That's a present for a friend, now give it back,"

The General waved what looked like a small silver cell phone over the box, smiled, saying, "My scan says, It's in here," and left the coffee shop.

Softy spoke into her communicators, saying, "The pigeon has the package."

Patsy asked, "What did you do to Lars?"

The General and half his crew just had an explosive end, and the Alliance's space force should be escorting what's left of Lars's ship back for trial."

Patsy stated, "Could you fill in the blanks,"

Softy stated, "When Jeff was at Moon Base One, Calistas devised a plan to take out the General and his ship with a bang. Because the package the General took from me contained a high explosive," Softy answered her cell phone, saying, "Yes, Sir, we are to be at thirty-six degrees west by 116 degrees north tomorrow at midnight."

At midnight in the middle of Death Valley, Softy stopped her four-wheeler, stepped out with Patsy and D-G, and made a campfire. Patsy inquired, "What are we doing in the middle of the desert,"

"You'll see," replied Softy.

A saucer ship weighing seventy-five thousand metric tons landed three hundred yards away then a grey-skinned humanoid with no visible external sex organs, ears, nose, and a slit for a mouth, slowly walked towards them. He shook Patsy's hand, saying, "I'm commander Noleck of the Time saucer ship Cassiopeia, pride of the Zamzummims fleet. I believe you have something that belongs to me,"

Patsy replied, "Yes, I do. But it's inside me."

Noleck spotted Patsy's thermos in the four-wheeler and questioned, "By any chance, is there coffee in that thermos? If so, I would love a cup because I haven't had a cup of earth-style coffee in a long time,"

Noleck sat by the women's campfire, enjoying his coffee, and told them about his adventures through time. He then brought Patsy into the saucer ship, carefully removed the alien computer through a delicate operation, then gave her a treasure chest full of gold for thanking Patsy for keeping the computer safe.

Back in the country bungalow on Legget Avenue. Patsy opened the wooden chest and stared at the gold doubloons that filled the it. Then she picked up a note that read in the Zamzummime language' Ui f lDi spojdftlpdN jl f I' ll f hi fs X ftf hpjohl plqrk! U hh f lffieQnp l ri f rtbefd Fbd lqrbf u xf lbelpo-lx jtrtof lEsi fdk bzgpn d f ln hjotr dhr -lLi boLi f lrtfdpof P odlxf lNdf opvhi lb Egpn lqrihJpolX firttq ohlpvdudq-lpo.

Patsy gave the note to Softy and asked, "What do you make of it? To me, it looks like a computer printer messed up,"

Softy stated, "It's written in the Zamzummim language, and it's a letter congratulating you and your friends,"

Epilogue

Patsy and the other Mandroids moved back to the Planetary Alliance and were greeted with honor for safely guarding the alien computer. Softy and D-G spoke to Thor, the Galaxy Sentinel, and he allowed them to live at the institute.

Patrick sat on Ocean Beach in California clad in a pair of black swim trunks with his wife Alexis who was clad in a one-piece Paisley bathing suit. He took a sip of his lemonade, stared at his wife, and asked, "Are you Doubleganger trying to fool me, or are you really my wife? Because I don't see any Freckles on your face."

Alexis giggled, removed the makeup from her face saying, "I was just teasing you. Now, how about a good swim before we head home to planet HP5."

When Thelma Jene Brideau was going to high school, she won an award for writing a poem. She thought it was great, but her writing talent was on the back burner, and never did anything with it.

In 2003 younger brother Gary T Brideau began to publish stories that inspired T. Jene Brideau to do something with her God-given talent, and she took up a course in writing to Polish her gift. But didn't have a chance to publish her work before she passed away. Below are the short stories that She wrote.

Short stories

by
T Jene Brideau

Peach Nuclear Poer

Michel de Nostradamus, born December 14, 1503, wrote several predictions concerning The New City. Most people believe it refers to New York. The Quatrain 49 was translated to read Garden of the new world near the new city, in the path of the hollow mountains. It will be seized and plunged into the Tub, forced to drink waters poisoned by sulfur. The Garden of the new world, I believe, refers to the state of New Jersey. It is known as the Garden State. Near the new city. It doesn't say in the new city; it says — near the new city. Many have thought this situation happened in New York and probably was 9-11. I believe this to be false. In the path of the hollow mountains is not the subway system in New York. The hollow mountains refer to a highway in Pennsylvania. I remember going through mountain after mountain after the mountain. At the end of that highway is the Peach Nuclear Plant. It will be seized and plunged into the tub; I believe this to be the nuclear tower. Forced to drink waters poisoned by sulfur. This is obviously radioactive fluid from the plant, poisoning the water and land. The tower is fueled by a liquid fluoride thorium reactor. The fusion of U-233 in the core heats molten carrier salt yellow. Nostradamus did not know of such things; he referred to it as sulfur: also, yellow. I wrote this because being forewarned is to be forearmed. NOW is the time to come to the aid of our Country.

The mystery by the beach

The sun was warm that day at the beach. Jane shuffled her feet through the soft beige sand looking for seashells. How warm and comforting it seemed. The wind blew slightly, rustling her light brown hair. Her toes combed the sand with every step. Unearthing an old brass key, she picked it up. A gleam of delight danced through her eyes at the find; she glanced around her, looking for someone who might have lost it. Jane looked up at the rocky shoreline to her right and then at the ever-rolling waves coming into the beach. There was no one. She slipped the key into her cut-off jeans and kept walking, looking for more treasures. Several prize seashells later, she glanced back at her funny footprints in the sand. Ja***ne decides to follow the water line back to her car. The air smelled of salt sea water and perfume to her, but to others, the smell of rotting fish. The water was cool on her bare feet as the sand seemed to be pulled away with each wave. Halfway back, she stopped again to examine the key she had found. It was highly unusual. The top was a beautiful ornate vine design, and the bottom was shaped like an old fashion key with just one tab on the end. She slipped it back into her pocket once again. "This will make a nice necklace," She thought. Too bad I won't have tiny earrings to match.

Looking up at the rocks, she could see a house on the rocks. It looked very old and worn. The white paint was hardly there, and the boards were gray and withered. Some windows were boarded up, while others were closed with shutters. Jane made her way up the rocky cliff to get a better look. Her bare feet hurt with every step. The house seemed to be abandoned or maybe just not opened up for the summer. Standing on the gray wooden porch, she tried the door, but it was locked. The door lock had the same design as the key she found on the beach. She took the key from her pocket. Slowly putting the key in the lock, she was surprised that it did indeed unlock the old door. Oh, she thought, what do I do now? She pushed on the door as it swung open. Seeing antique furniture peeking out from under large white sheets, she moved about the room in absolute awe. The old red carpet was a welcomed sight for her scraped and aching feet. She stood in front of a large picture over a stone fireplace. The woman was very old and seemed to be almost smiling. She was dressed in a navy blue dress with white buttons down the front. Her high collar seemed to hide an array of wrinkles. Her gray hair was swirled upwards to encircle the top of her head. Mesmerized by the picture, Jane wondered who she was and how did things get into such a rundown state. She sat in one of the dining room chairs in another room, imagining how it must have felt to eat in China, using silver utensils and drinking out of crystal glasses. How elegant things must have been many years ago? She suddenly felt sad thinking of the old woman who probably died years ago with no one to care for her home.

Feeling a bit tired, she made her way to a nice comfortable chair by the old stone fireplace, looking up at the old woman's picture, her eyes slowly closed as she drifted off to sleep.

"Okay, who are you, and what are you doing here!" came a voice sharp enough to wake Jane. "I was just looking around. I'm sorry, I didn't disturb anything except maybe this chair," she replied meekly. She looked up to see a middle-aged man frowning down at her with piercing blue eyes.

"I should have you arrested for trespassing. You can't wander into someone's house just 'cause ya feel like it!" he shouted.

"Again, I'm sorry I meant no harm. I was just curious and

"I don't care! You get out of here before I take a poker to ya!" he shouted. This time he seemed a bit interested in who she was.

"Okay, I'm going. Just keep your shirt on," replied Jane.

"If you walk around to the front, you will see there's a path. I see your feet are all scratched. I'm assuming you came up the rocks out back."

"I'm going," Jane answered. Slinking past the man and toward the front door. "Wait a minute, who are you, and what are you doing here," she questioned, folding her arms and demanding an answer.

"I'm a neighborhood security - - person. Someone called me to let me know that the door was wide open." he stammered.

"0, yeah, what's your name? I'm gonna check on you. Maybe you are trespassing too." "My name is Mike Owiship."

"What kinda name is that? Sounds phony to me." she snickered.

"My name is Jane, and that's all you'll get out of me. I'm going, but I'll be back to check on you." "Fine," he sneered as he turned to walk away.

"Fine," Jane replied while walking swiftly to the opened front door.

Jane walked around the house trying to peer in a crack in the shutters, but there were none to be found. Disappointed, she walked slowly to her Aqua Blue car.

"Not a bad-looking guy," she pondered as she patted the key in her pocket. "I'll be back. This is too interesting to let go."

Chloe's Surprise Adventure

It was early morning as Chloe stood in the open sliding glass door of her studio apartment. The dew glistened on the wet grass as she gazed up the hill to a road far above. A rising morning mist revealed a bright sun and the promise of a wonderful day. Newly retired, Chloe relished every moment of every day. She glanced down at her brightly colored cup and then up at her newly polished red sports car parked across the little side street. She smiled and took a sip of her special brew. Looking up to the top of the hill, she saw an eighteen-wheeler barreling down the road. The road had a sharp turn at the end, but the truck wasn't slowing down. It was exceptionally unusual to see trucks on that stretch of road. She watched as the partially rusted yellow hooded truck whizzed past the turn skidding straight down the hill toward her while the trailer seemed to slide off sideways. Chloe watched in horror as the silver trailer with large circular openings tumbled violently down the hill. The side of the trailer snapped open, throwing horses in every direction. Try as they would, the horses could not get to their feet. They rolled down the hill next to the trailer. The driver was ejected from the cab. He struggled to his feet and ran wildly past her window. The cab remained on the side of the hill while the twisted metal trailer continued its cascading, landing on top of her newly acquired car (running in tiptop condition), gleaming in its freshly waxed job. In seconds that twisted hunk of metal wiped out her dream car, which she had worked so hard for. She couldn't watch any longer. She felt guilty, feeling sorry for herself as she gazed out over such horror. Chloe's eyes filled with tears as her knees grew weak from the gruesome incident. Several of the horses were not moving, while others found their footing and went racing into the countryside. One black horse went galloping right past her sliding glass door. Startled, she jumped back, almost falling to the floor. She grabbed the gold paisley-print curtain and slowly pulled herself up. It seemed like hours, but it had only been minutes. Fire trucks and ambulances came out of nowhere. The paramedics checked the downed horses while some stood near them waiting for, she assumed, a veterinarian. Finally, they showed up to check the fallen horses. They still weren't moving. Chloe turned away so she wouldn't have to watch the vet putting the last of the horses down. Slowly the field was emptied, but the twisted metal still lay on top of her car. Then a tow truck backed up to the wreckage and pulled everything away. She could look no longer. Lowering her head, she walked away from the sliding glass door, leaving it open. A man in uniform appeared, handing her a business card. She looked up to see a mechanic in greasy overalls. He seemed out of breath and anxious. "Lady, if you want your car, it will be at Big Al's garage. You, okay?"

"Ask me tomorrow. I gotta sit down before I pass out." Her head was spinning as she tried to process what had just happened in the blink of an eye.

"Right," he stammered. "Gotta go." He added, "Did you see that whole thing? Wow! What a mess." He searched her face for a response. Not finding one, he added, "Right....again.... gotta go."

She made her way to the small round kitchen table, placing the card before her. After calling her insurance agent, she took a local bus to Al's Garage. The garage smelled of the usual oil and grease, and a strange smell of apples filled the air.

"Can I help you?" came a voice from the doorway. An older man, she guessed must be Al, came in from the bake of the shop.

"Yes, I'm the lady who had her car smashed this morning,"

"Oh, what a mess. It must have been a spectacular accident. I heard all about it. Sorry, Ma'am, but that car is now a pile of tin. Totaled, definitely totaled! However, if you're interested in something else, say a compact car, I have a nice selection in my lot. Do you have any money to spend?"

"Well, I was just on the way to the bank. I have four hundred I could put down on one until I get a check from my insurance,"

"Right over here is a nice little white Honda. I can let you have that one for four hundred down. She runs well, just came here for a tune-up."

After checking the car over, Chloe decided it would have to do. She handed him the four hundred dollars. He smiled kindly at her. "I'll be back with your receipt,"

She sat in the driver's seat, playing with the controls while she waited for him to return.

"Excuse me, miss, but you are sitting in my car," came a woman's voice at the window.

"You must be mistaken," she stammered. "I just purchased this car from the garage."

"Sorry, but this is my car. To prove it, I have another set of keys right here. I just brought this car in for a tune-up."

"I'm so sorry, but I just gave the man a down payment on this car."

"I think he's made a mistake. You need to go talk to him," replied the woman. Chloe made her way back to the garage office. "Excuse me, but I just gave you four hundred dollars down payment on that white car in the lot. The woman says it's her car. You must have sold me the wrong one."

"Sorry, lady, I don't know what you're talking about," he replied sharply. "You never gave me any money."

"Yes, I did," she screamed. "I'm gonna call a cop. You are nothing but a swindler!"

"Get out of here; I have work to do," he ordered as he slammed the door shut. Chloe's eyes filled with tears. More unexpected turn of events to deal with. She slowly walked away from the garage, trying to see where she was going.

"I saw the whole thing. He's as dishonest as they come. I can help you. I'm an assistant to the police."

Chloe looked up to see a young woman dressed in a full white Indian maiden outfit. She could see tall white boots with a fringe on the top. The turquoise beading was particularly beautiful. Her brown skin showed above the boots.

"You can go down to the police station and at least file a report. I know of several others he has swindled in the past. Take the license plate number of that white car with you."

Chloe managed a smile and thanked her for her advice.

The next stop is the police headquarters. What a predicament. How could she have lost two cars in one day? Heading downtown, Chloe had a chance to reflect. She knew they wouldn't believe her, but at least she could file a police report.

"I want to file a police report, officer," She stated to the policeman behind the desk. "I've been robbed."00

"Okay, fill out this report." He handed her a sheet to fill out. "I'll be with you in a minute."

She did as he asked, paying attention to every detail. She even listed the license plate of the little white Honda.

"You got any proof, lady?" asked the Officer.

"No, he never gave me my receipt."

"Sorry, but you'll have to take him to court," he replied gruffly. "This is a civil matter."

Chloe made her way down to the lobby, where she could take the bus home. She felt disillusioned and drained from her experiences. Standing in the lobby, Chloe noticed a woman in a long gray trench coat carrying a large black garbage bag in one hand and a dog carrier in the other.

"Can I help you?" she asked. "You looked confused.

"Do you know if I can catch the Number 7 bus here," the woman said softly. Before Chloe could answer, the woman walked briskly out the door. She glanced back briefly at Chloe with a frown. Dropping both the bag and the dog carrier, she ran down the street, disappearing into the crowd. Chloe rushed out the door, her eyes searching wildly for the woman. There were only people getting on and off buses. Chloe picked up the black plastic bag. It was surprisingly light. She peered inside to see a handmade quilt. She picked up the dog carrier next. There seemed to be something inside. She opened the zipper carefully. "Oh, my," she gasped. "It's a—a baby. Oh, no," she whimpered.

"Now what!"

Chloe waited for an hour or so, but the lady never returned. "She knew she should probably report this to the police since she was already there, but she did not want to. If the woman wanted the police to have it, she would have left it with them." She peered inside again. A baby girl, I've always wanted a baby girl." she smiled. Home again. What a welcomed sight! She had purchased all the necessary items she thought she might need for the baby. "I need to name you something," she cooed to the little

114

girl. "Baby just won't do. I think I will call you Susie. I don't know anyone by that name, but I like it." She giggled.

Chloe quickly made arrangements for a neighbor to watch Susie. She had to try and find the woman who had left her behind. She arrived back at the spot where she last saw her. She waited for bus number seven. "Aha, there it is," she whispered. Stepping onto the stairs, she shouted to the driver. "Excuse me, have you ever seen a tall thin woman wearing a gray trench coat? She might have been carrying a large black garbage bag and a dog carrier. She asked about the Number 7 bus.

"You're in luck. I did see her this morning," the driver said. "I dropped her off right here. She acted so weirdly. That's why I remembered her.

"Do you know where she lives or where you picked her up? I have something of hers I'd like to return."

"Sure, I can point you in the right direction," he smiled. "Get on the bus, and I will show you where she got on."

Chloe was on her way. This was truly an adventure. Her stomach was churning from excitement. How could anyone leave behind a baby?

"This is your stop. I believe she lives over there in that run-down old apartment house. Please be careful," the driver warned. "This is not a nice neighborhood."

Chloe made her way over to the tall brick building. The door creaked as she opened it. She carefully checked the names on the mailboxes, but nothing stood out. She turned to see the Manager tacked on the first door. Poking her head inside, she shouted, "Hello, anyone here?"

A short fat woman smoking a cigarette came to the front desk. "Yeah, what ya want, lady," She looked Chloe up and down.

"I'm looking for a lady who wears a long gray trench coat. I was told she lives here. I have something to give her."

"I'll take it off your hands, sweetie; I know her well," she smirked.

"No, I have to give it to her personally. Which is her apartment."

"Well, normally I would say no, but. . . you seem like an honest person.

She's right down here in 3B. I'll take you myself. Shirley, watch the desk," she yelled over her shoulder. "I will be right back."

"Well, this is it," she announced, opening the door.

Chloe stood there searching the room for something to tell her who the mystery woman was. The room was barren of furniture except for a small mail-filled table. As she sifted through the stack, she realized this woman had at least twelve different names. Were they hers, or did she steal other people's mail? Chloe turned to the woman still standing in the doorway. "What is her name," she asked excitedly. "Are these all for her?"

The woman just glared back and said nothing. "Come dear; I've gotta get back to the desk. Sorry, I can't help you. You see, it's cash only here. No names."

Chloe made her way out to the street, disappointed and troubled. Out of the corner of her eye, she could see three bikers staring at her as she walked down the block. She could see them turn and walk toward her. She quickened her step, and so did they.

Chloe was scared to turn around, ran to the next street as fast as she could. She glanced back. They were still there and closing in on her. She was desperate. "Hey, lady, what's your hurry?" They all laughed.

Looking ahead, she saw an Army caravan. A Jeep with an officer was at the wheel.

"Sir, please wait," Chloe cried frantically. "I'm being chased by three bikers.

Please help me!"

"All stop!" yelled the Captain. "Sorry, miss, we really are not allowed to pick up civilians," he shouted. "But since I see those bikers, apparently after you, we can make an exception. Climb in and hurry."

Chloe told her whole story to the Captain at record speed. She was bursting at the seams to get back to the baby. This wasn't what she expected in her wildest dreams.

"I've already lost two cars today, long story, and almost mugged. You're a lifesaver."

"I'm so glad I met you," breathed the Captain. "It just so happens that I have a car you can have. I was going to give it to the charity here in town, but I'd rather give it to you."

The convoy entered the base through the back entrance to park all the trucks and jeeps.

"Show this pass at the front gate. I will call them and let them know you are on your way. You will find the car in the big parking lot to the left. The papers are in the glove compartment. Here's the key. Press this tab, and the door will unlock. If you have any problems with it, my name is on the registration. Good luck. I hope things will get better for you.

Walking over to the parking lot, Chloe smiled to herself. Maybe things will get better. She stopped short in front of row after row of green cars, green Jeeps, and green ATVs. Which was her car? She remembered that the captain said to press the little button on the key. There it is. Just in front of her, a door swung open. Well, that was easy. I hope I can drive this green monster. It was bigger than she was used to. Climbing inside, she was confused. Where was the steering wheel? Where was the ignition? This did not look right. She buckled the seat belt, which closed the door as the interior lights came on.

"Destination, please," came a voice from the dash. Lights twinkle everywhere.

"Destination, please," came the voice again.

"Please take me to 121 Blueberry Drive," she replied with great hesitation.

Immediately the engine whirled as it ascended ten feet in the air. It made a quick turn, landed, and stopped next to the guardhouse.

"Pass, please," requested the Officer of the Day.

She quickly held it up as the car moved slowly through the gate. Once outside the gate, the engine seems to quiet down. Again, the car lifted off the ground and hesitated for only a moment before it flew across town. Coming to a stop, the car's voice announced, "Your destination is complete."

Chloe opened her eyes to see herself sitting in front of her apartment.

"Wow! What a rush. From the sublime to the ridiculous. I certainly didn't expect this."

Rushing inside, she found it hard to keep from coming apart. The baby was sleeping peacefully as she gazed at the little figure. How cute she was. It had been a long time since she had been anywhere near a baby.

"You'll never guess what happened to me," She said to the neighbor who had been babysitting. "It was the most exciting, worst, best day ever. I'll explain tomorrow."

"You'd better tell me because I am dying to know," demanded her neighbor. "You can't just leave me hanging like this. See you bright and early tomorrow for coffee, promise?"

"I promised; now go, and thanks a million."

As the neighbor left her apartment, Chloe sank deep into her oversized recliner, only rising when she heard a loud knock on her sliding-glass door. There stood an Army soldier staring intently into the room. Opening the door, she heard,

"Miss, the car you rode home in, is a top-secret experiment. The Captain gave you the wrong keys. I would strongly suggest that you mention this to no one. You will find the car promised to you outside. Please give me the keys you have," demanded the soldier.

"You mean I don't get to keep that flying car?"

"Absolutely not. That car should not have left the base."

Chloe glanced at the other green car across the tiny street. "That's the car? I thank you for your generosity, and I am glad to give the other one back.

Here are the keys. Again, I am thankful for any car." She smiled as they exchanged keys. Turning around, she was surprised to see the woman in the long gray coat glaring back at her.

"What the. .... I mean, how did you find me, and how did you get in here? I've been looking for you. What's going on?" Suddenly Chloe was concerned for little Susie.

"I am in need of your help. I've been running, and I am tired of it. Can I trust you? Of course, I can," the woman continued. "I am being deported back to France. My little Bridget is the most important thing to me. I must leave her here. She was born here in this country. I want her to stay in this country where things are good."

"Why? When. What about her birth certificate? How can I keep her?"

"Her birth certificate is on the side of the carrier. Please, I trust you. I was going to leave her at the police station, but I just couldn't. One more thing — as she grows up, just tell her you're her aunt. That way, if I can come back, she will accept me as her mother. I only want the best for her," she pleaded. Will you help me?"

"Of course," Chloe replied. "I will take a chance and will try to help you."

"No, do not try; just do, and you will be fine," replied the woman.

"What is your name?" asked Chloe.

"All the information is on the papers in the carrier. I must go. I don't know if anyone has followed me here or not. I was frightened when I saw that soldier in the window, but now, I feel everything will be fine," the lady smiled. "I must go." She rushed past Chloe and was out the front door in an instant. Chloe sank back down into her oversized recliner. There was so much to consider. There were so many plans to make. Clouds were forming outside as lightning lit up the sky. She walked cautiously toward the glass door. The lightning seemed more violent than before. The rain was now pouring down as rivers formed in the street. A trash can thumped down the covered street. She could hear the howling as the lightning lit up the night. Just then, there was another bright flash.

Chloe gasped as she bolted upright in her bed. Was it storming? How did she get in bed? Realizing all that had happened was a dream, she sighed a big sigh of relief. Thank heavens, I was dreaming. Grabbing her bathrobe, she ran to the glass door. Peering out, she saw her little red sports car. "My car, my car, it's Okay," she screamed. "I am so glad I have my little red sports car. I may never be the same." She twirled around to pour herself a cup of coffee already programmed in the coffee pot the night before and walked leisurely back to the glass door. The morning mist was rising from the hill as the sun slowly rose in the sky.

Chloe glanced up at the highway at the top of the hill. An eighteen-wheeler was speeding down the road. It had a yellow hooded and partially rusted cab, just as it was in her dream.

The Peril's of Water

It was the middle of summer in a tiny town in Canada. Almost unbelievable to my family, I remembered things at the age of one. My first memory was in the summer of 1946. My Dad traveled a lot in the Merchant Marines and was relaxing at home. He was getting restless -being home for about a month. "Let's go on a picnic. It's a beautiful day with no clouds in sight," he announced. My Mum agreed, busy thinking of how much work it would take to get everything together. She packed a lunch -I don't remember what- and several blankets. We headed to my Nana's house, which stood on top of a hill by the bay. A small island was just offshore, beckoning to our little group.

My brothers and my aunt were also waiting to enjoy the day. They waved from the front porch with blankets and a large picnic basket in their arms.

We all merrily walked down the hill to the shore, talking and laughing gleefully.

My Dad pulled the rowboat ashore, holding it steady for my Aunt and my Nana, and one brother to climb on board. "I'll be right back," he yelled. Rowing away From the shore. "I can't take all of you this time."

It seemed like an eternity, but he was smiling and holding the boat for the rest of us. "I want you to remain very still; we could tip over, sooo, no moving around." He looked straight at me. I could see the concerned look on his face, so I knew he was serious.

Mum sat at the back of the boat, holding me in her arms. I froze, scared to breathe. What was this water stuff anyway? Mum kept telling me to be very still. I could tell she was nervous, so the situation must be serious.

Finally, we were all gathered together on the tiny island. It was only about a square acre in size. We all breathed a sigh of relief as Mum and my aunt spread the blankets. That was the first day I became aware of the big ocean. It was love at first sight. Being totally fascinated by this strange stuff, I was off to explore. I crawled to the water's edge, ignoring the pebbles under my knees. It was certainly a mystery to me. I balanced myself on my left hand while splashing in the water with my right. I couldn't understand why I could put my hand into something that looked solid. I continued to splash until suddenly, my arm grew weak. Try as I might, I couldn't hold myself up. I fell face-first into the water. Out of nowhere, my Mum scooped me up and placed me back on the blanket. However, my thoughts were still wandering about that strange substance. I waited until Mum's back was turned and crawled back down to the water. I scurried as fast as I could, but I never did make it back down to the water. Mum was exhausted by the end of the day. I had turned a beautiful day into a "catch me if you can, game." Mum and Dad agreed that it would be a long time before they would take me on another island picnic.

Time passed quickly. I was about four years old. One summer day, just before lunch, Mum asked me to take a big bag of sandwiches to some men working in the field. She warned me, "DON'T PICK THE FLOWERS!"

In those days, everyone pitched in to help each other, cutting grass, chopping wood, or whatever needed to be done, all for the price of lunch. It was more like a potluck. The men worked while the women cooked.

It was a long walk down a country road full of rocks and dirt. As I rounded a bend in the road, I saw several men sitting down, taking a break in the noonday sun. "My mum told me to bring you these sandwiches," I said shyly.

One man stood up, took the bag, and passed out the sandwiches. I was busily eyeing all the pretty dandelions by the side of the river.

"Don't fall in the water," they laughed.

"The flowers were already cut down. A few wouldn't hurt." I thought, starting to pick up some flowers.

One of the men asked, "Are those flowers for your mum?"

"Yes," I told them with a big smile.

All the men started to pick up as many dandelions as they could.

"Here you go," smiled one of them. "Hold out your arms so I can hand them to you."

I did as he asked. There were so many I could hardly hold them. After all, I didn't pick any. "Mum will love these. It will make her very happy," I murmured, running home as fast as I could.

"Mum, look what I got for you," I announced, bursting with pride. I was elated to do something nice for her.

She took one look at those flowers and screamed, "I told you NOT to pick any flowers." She batted the flowers out of my arms and sent me to my room to change. After a quick bath, I was sent to the downstairs spare room. My room was at the top of the stairs. I didn't question it. I was too devastated to ask why.

That night I could hardly breathe. My gasping sounds filled the house. I didn't connect the beautiful flowers to my extremely labored breathing.

As I lay there, I heard a knock at the door. I knew it was late because it was dark outside. I could hear Mum talking to a man. It wasn't a voice that I recognized. His voice was soft and rather soothing.

Mum opened the door to the room while the man placed a funny-looking machine on the floor. "Here, put some of this on her pillow and some on her handkerchief. If you put some of this inside the machine, it will fill the air. I'm sure she will feel better soon."

My Mum did as he instructed.

I could feel some relief almost immediately as they both left the room. I tried to rest I was exhausted from breathing so hard. They both reappeared in the doorway sometime later.

"She's breathing better already. I don't hear her gasping for air anymore."

Mum said, relieved.

I smiled at her news.

"I can leave the vacuum overnight if you wish," he offered.

"That would be wonderful," she whispered, thinking that I was asleep. "If this works, I will certainly buy your vacuum cleaner," she promised.

"So that's what it was. A vacuum cleaner. What's a vacuum cleaner? Do we even need something called a vacuum to clean?" Wonderment filled my thoughts as I drifted off to sleep. The next day I was fully recovered. The Electrolux Vacuum cleaner salesman returned. Mum kept her word. She bought the machine and all the attachments. Word spread through the town like wildfire. No one had ever seen a vacuum before. People came from all around to see this wonderful machine. Because of his good deed, he was well rewarded. The fluid was the oil of eucalyptus. What are the odds a vacuum cleaner salesman would be carrying just what I needed and calling at that exact time I needed it? I still keep a bottle on hand. Why take a chance? He might not come calling next time. That was a disastrous summer for me. I was constantly getting into trouble. My two brothers and I were playing hide and seek or whatever silly games we could think of. My brothers kept running in and out of the house for one reason or another while I waited patiently outside.

Sometimes we would just lay on an old cowhide, watching the clouds. Mum told us it was from a buffalo which made it more exciting.

Later that day, I grew extremely thirsty. Unlike my brothers, I hadn't been running in and out of the house 20 times an hour. I just wanted a nice refreshing glass of cold water. I'd been out all day, never once going inside for a drink. It was not to be. Mum was busy washing the kitchen floor. Plead as I might, she would not let me in.

"You've been running in and out all day. I just washed the floor, and it's still wet. Come back in a little while."

I pouted, then decided I would find my own water someplace else. Walking along the side of the road, I saw water flowing down the ditch. I knelt down to take a closer look. It looked Chrystal clear. I determined it was safe to drink and had my fill.

The next day I awoke uncommonly weak. I could hardly stand and was rushed to the hospital. I don't remember how I got there. I became delirious and tried to get dressed, putting my underwear on my head. The nurse found me and put me back to bed. After that, my clothes and shoes mysteriously disappeared. The next day I awoke cold and quite embarrassed because I lay totally naked. My bed was surrounded by doctors and nurses and was trying to decide what was wrong with me and why was my whole body covered in big red blotches. I was elated when they finally decided to cover me. In desperation, they decided I must have Typhoid fever, and I was promptly Quarantined. They gave me some orange liquid which I promptly returned. They were armed with plenty of needles and all sorts of devices I had never seen before. The nights were long, and I cried through most of them. I remember one of the more painful situations was when the nurse decided to push the cuticle back on my fingers. I hated that. It was my 5th birthday. Here I was, stuck in the hospital. My Mum couldn't even visit me. She'd wave from the doorway to let me know she was there. If they had asked me, I could have told them what happened. They never asked, so I kept quiet and eventually recovered. The hospital records said, "Illness unknown."

When I arrived home, Mum had made my favorite cake. Chocolate with hot fudge topped and five candles. Sadly, I had to give all my comic books to my brothers. I don't know how long I was in the hospital, but the comic book pile was at least a foot high. Years passed, I never told anyone what really happened, and as time went on, it didn't matter.

Mum eventually grew tired of waiting for Dad's yearly visit. They talked it over and decided to move to a big city in Connecticut. The house was sold with everything in it to some distant relative. I felt perplexed and anxious, but the choice had been made.

Dad made all the arrangements, and in a short time, we were on our way At the border between the United States and Canada, something went wrong. We had to sit in the office while Mum and Dad were taken to another room. An excruciating hour later, they emerged, looking like two lost souls.

"Sorry, kids, but we have to go back. We don't have the proper papers. It's just for a short time," declared Mum.

"We can't go back; we have no place to go and no place to sleep." protested my two brothers and me.

"It will only be for a few days," Mum cried, trying to comfort us. There were hugs all around as we made our way back to the car and onto Nana's house.'

We were greeted with a banquet of food and a house full of family members all talking at once. The smell of baked beans and freshly baked apple pie filled my senses. The days flew by in a whirl of disarray. So much to absorb in such a short time.

Three days later, the papers were ready. We were cleared to venture out once more. This time we were going by train to the ship docked at Yarmouth, Nova Scotia. I remember standing on the platform, looking up at this monstrous train. It seemed so high I couldn't see the top in the blackness of the night. I think I screamed, which brought a conductor running towards us. He was kind and reassured us that it was nothing to be afraid of. I whimpered as he held my hand to help me up the stairs ahead of us. It seemed like a big living room as I stepped into one of the seats. I promptly curled up and exhausted and soon fell asleep next to my two brothers. It was a short trip, and soon we were unloading again. It was still night, and we made our way down to the wharf to catch the next ship sailing to the U.S.

Once on board, we were herded to a huge room called a lounge. It was night, and all I wanted to do was go to bed, but there were only long tufted red seats. Dad left momentarily and returned in a hurry. "We're in for it," he declared.

"I was just up at the bar. They are covering the bar with wet towels."

"What does that mean," Mum asked.

"It means we're in for a big storm. It's gonna get rough. They put wet towels down to keep things from sliding around." He reached into his pocket and gave us all a little white pill.

Later that night, I had to go to the bathroom. Mum took my hand and led me to the big ladies' room. We were horrified at what we saw. Everyone must have had Spaghetti for dinner. There was sauce and noodles everywhere. It looked like something out of a nightmare. Mum checked every stall, but they were all a disgusting mess. To my surprise, she quickly cleaned off a corner of a sink, propping me on the edge. Everyone was too sick to care.

When we got back to the lounge, everyone was wide awake. Dad offered us a tour of the ship. He was excited to share his knowledge of the different decks. I was the only one willing to go. It was a great tour and a special moment with my Dad. Making our way back to the lounge, we saw a sailor coming down the stairs. The ship pitched forward, and he went crashing to the floor. Dad laughed so hard he was bent over, much to the embarrassment of the sailor. "He couldn't have been a sailor very long," he bellowed. "Everyone on a ship knows you walk down backward to have a better grip."

We made it through the storm without sinking. There we were, tired and hungry but excited to be on our way. My uncle picked us up in his car. Once again, we were on our way. Only five more hours until we reached our new apartment and new life in the big city.

THE END

Predictions

The future is a space in time that has not happened. Yet, people try to guess, wish, and pray that it will favor them. Prophets have been predicting the future for centuries. I am sure even the cavemen wondered, what will tomorrow bring? What fish will they catch, or what animal will they kill for dinner? They might have wondered if it would rain or if a storm was on the horizon. All these things are questions of the future. We still have these questions today in our everyday lives. Most of them are usually answered except the weatherman, who is seldom right. There are times when I hope he is wrong. What teenager hasn't worried about who will be their date? Who will be their friend after High School? Who will they marry, and how many children will they have. What will they have to look forward to? How many catastrophes will they have to endure? What occupation should they choose? Everything is in the future. Of course, the questions are all answered in time. Not always as we think.

When we get old, we wonder, how long do I have? What will my health be like? Will I be able to live on my own? Where will the money come from? All questions of future events of everyday living. It is human nature to wonder and plan for common things. It is very difficult to prepare for the unknown. That is why some are competitively seeking answers to questions that haven't been asked yet. There are ancient prophecies, world prophecies, and prophecies in every culture back to the beginning of time. There are some that chart the stars by the way they move in the night sky. They seek to predict what will become of us. Their equipment was simple. High-powered telescopes were not available as they are today. Hundreds of years ago, the sky was much different than the sky we see today. The stars have changed their positions from where they were hundreds of years ago. It has also been rumored that a great meteor will hit the Earth. Will we be able to reflect it? I think they're still working on that.

Some have visions of future events. They see pictures in their mind. The visions are not always understood. It's more like a jigsaw puzzle - trying to make the pieces fit. The psychics who help solve murder cases see numbers, objects, and places. Putting all the clues together to mean something is difficult, even for the person seeing the vision. Whatever the technique, it was charged with anxiety to know what lies ahead for themselves or others. Sometimes visions come in the middle of the night without warning. I have read many prophecies of a man named Michel de Nostradamus, who was born on December 14, 1503. His knowledge and the way he thought was not excepted in those days. He was an unappreciated visionary of his time. He wrote what is called "Quatrains." His look into the future. In several of these "Quatrains," he mentions a place called the New City. It is common knowledge the name refers to New York City.

I read a Quatrain that I knew was of interest to many, especially in the East. If you live in New York City or the surrounding states, it will raise more attention than it would on the west coast.

One of these Quatrains I knew exactly what meant. I told several people who were also curious about the meaning. I also told a person of authority. They told me to say nothing while others laughed and disregarded it completely.

One prominent friend was extremely upset that I wanted to reveal a different conclusion than already stated by authors who have written books on the life and times of Nostradamus. I was warned to say nothing for fear my interpretation would give those who would harm us ideas.

I was devastated but agreed to say nothing. I didn't want anything to happen because of what I knew. This was 20 years ago. Putting this idea out of my mind was seriously affecting my everyday living. Having read so many other prophecies took its toll on me. I was afraid to face another day, terrified another day wouldn't exist. I tried to keep busy with new activities but to no avail; two years passed. I convinced myself to live for the present. If tomorrow isn't there for me, then so be it. I slowly accepted the idea of saying nothing.

Recently a fellow writer wrote about the end of the world. What would happen to us and to our children? I immediately recoiled and fled. I did not want to think of all those prophecies I managed to put behind me. It was too late. All the prophecies came flooding back, taunting me, pulling me back to when I had first studied Nostradamus 20 years earlier. Sleep was not forthcoming. I awoke every few hours. My appetite was slight. I felt stressed with no way out. I wandered around the house, rearranging furniture. (My favorite thing to do when I'm upset). I talked on the phone for hours. I visited friends and went shopping to fill my day. There was only one answer. I would have to write about the one thing I was warned not to. The interpretation, I felt, had to be told.

Many writers have associated Quatrain forty-nine with the disastrous day of 911. I don't think that was it. All the pieces do not fit. That catastrophe was truly a blow to thousands and affected the lives of all of us. Security was tightened in all the airports. Background checks were questioned more closely. People became scared of what was to come next. Especially the people in the East near New York. Life went on with a cautious state of mind. I'm sure when Mt. St. Helen's blew, the west coast was devastated. It took weeks to clear the roads and the dust from cars. Their belongings were destroyed, not to mention the lives that were lost. The effect was not as severe in the East. They felt sympathy for those in Washington but could not possibly know how it felt to be dumped on by a blanket of ash. In order to properly interpret Quatrain 49, it is necessary to know the east coast and where things are. You can't find an address unless you know the street and which town it is in. Knowing the areas it mentioned, it wasn't hard for me to put things all together. The Quatrain was translated to read:

Garden of the new world near the new city, In the path of the hollow mountains: It will be seized and plunged into the Tub, Forced to drink waters poisoned by sulfur

"Garden of the new world," I believe, refers to New Jersey. New Jersey is called "The Garden State" because Abraham Browning of Camden, In his address, compared New Jersey to an immense barrel filled with good things to eat and open at both ends, Pennsylvanians grabbing from one end and New Yorkers from the other. He called New Jersey the "Garden State," and the name has clung to it ever since.

Next, it says, "Near the new city." It doesn't say it takes place in New

York. It says, (keyword), NEAR the new city. So that means the disaster does not take place in New York at all, only near it.

"In the path of the hollow mountains" I have read many versions of this sentence. Some say that they think it refers to the Holland Tunnel and the

Brooklyn Tunnel in New York and/or the subway systems below ground which are extensive. However, it does say near, not in the new city.

I believe the hollow mountains mentioned are beyond New York and New Jersey. They are the mountains of Pennsylvania. When I was young, I remember visiting someone in Pennsylvania. I don't remember who, but I remember those tunnels that go through the mountains. There were so many of them—tunnel after tunnel after tunnel. I didn't think I was going to make it out alive. The exhaust fumes that built up inside the tunnels were unbearable. I tried to cover my nose each time we went through a tunnel. After every tunnel, we rolled down the windows to get some fresh air. I was elated to reach our destination. Unfortunately, we had to return the same way. I never went there again.

"It will be seized and plunged into the tub." This, too, is clear as crystal. At the end of that highway is a nuclear plant called The Peach Nuclear Plant. Our enemy will seize the plant in a way not yet known and destroy the facility. The Tub refers to the nuclear tower. The tower is fueled by a yellow liquid which is radioactive. Liquid fluoride thorium reactor. The fusion of U-233 in the core heats molten carrier salt (yellow).

"Forced to drink water poisoned by sulfur" is obviously the radioactive fluid from the plant poisoning a great deal of our land. I believe Nostradamus did not recognize the fluid as radioactive but could only describe it as sulfur, which is the only substance he knew. Sulfur is yellow in color.

I know that if this does happen, it will be an even bigger catastrophe than 911. The land will be contaminated for years. Many people will lose everything they own and even their lives. It will become another "Chernobyl." Power will be lost for thousands of people. They will never be able to return to their homes if they survive the event. Can this happen in the US.? We hope not. However, forewarned is forearmed. If we know in advance, we can prevent the disaster. Unfortunately, we don't know the hour or those that will cause it,

Although many new safety features have been installed and the "tub" is extremely thick concrete, it can still be sabotaged and destroyed.

The reason I decided to write this version of the interpreted Quatrain is to warn those powers that be. If they will take this seriously, then maybe we can prevent another disaster; knowledge in advance is an invaluable tool. Had the Titanic been forewarned, it would still be sailing today. If we were forewarned, 911 would not have happened.

Even the strongest threshold can be destroyed from the inside out. The enemy does not always strike from the outside in. Case in point — The Trojan Horse. Nostradamus was truly a man of vision. One can only hope that these events will never take place. Talking with him would be a big event even today. The validity of all of his predictions is subject to interpretation. The fascination of all his predictions is greatly valued today. There is a prediction of his that says, "The up shall be down, and the down shall be up." This is a prediction that, eventually, the world will be upside down. What will cause such a fate?

We can ponder over many a prediction and coming disasters, but, If we live each day to the fullest, then we will have no regrets. I believe there will be a tomorrow even after such a dreadful disaster. Man has always survived. Nothing is certain even though we want to know future events; it is sometimes better not to know. The anxiety that would build in you would be unbearable. Every thought would be of that day rather than living for the day already given you.

God gave us a clue of what is to come in the bible, but only He knows when things will take place. Since He is all-knowing and all-seeing, I, for one, leave everything to His good judgment.

HOME IS ONLY A NEW YEAR AWAY

A new year begins again
but still, things seem the same.
With old friends by your side
and new ones in the game
Time goes on and yet stands still
how mystifying and bizarre
you wish your family could be here
instead of off so far.
Soon all will fall into place
as life goes round and round
when the new year comes again
you might be homeward bound.

Why Did The Light Bulb Blow Out

"Hey, George, would you change the light bulb in the area over the stove? The light bulbs are in the closet in the laundry room. I put them there because they are easier to reach. I've got to make dinner, so please hurry. While you're at it, take the beef out of the refrigerator. I'm going to the store to get some carrots for the stew. Don't be eating any of that leftover apple pie; that's our dessert. Do you hear me?" Martha yelled from the front hallway by the front door.

"Yes, I heard you; change the light bulb so you can see what you are cooking. Not that that would help any," he muttered.

What was that George? Just saying I don't need any help, dear. See you when you get back."

George sundered out to the laundry room to get the light bulb. Let's see; we have forty watts, sixty watts, seventy-five-watt, and one hundred watts. I think I'll put in the one hundred watts. That should light up the whole kitchen." George hurried back to the kitchen and put in his choice of bulb. Once finished, he took the stew beef out of the refrigerator and threw it on the counter. "I think I'd better go do something else before I have something else to do.' he scoffed.

George made his way to the living room to relax in his favorite recliner to check the sports page in the daily paper.

Martha came home a few minutes later. "I sure hope that light bulbs are in," she stated.

"Why sure, it's all set," George announced.

"OK, I'll start dinner; got some nice rolls too. You didn't eat the pie, did you?'

"flaw," he grunted, not looking up from his paper.

Sometime later, Martha came into the living room to rest for a bit.

"Dinner's on, the salad is made, and the stew will be ready in about ten minutes."

Suddenly there was a large POP from the kitchen.

"What was that" shouted George.

"I don't know, but we'd better check." Cried, Martha.

They both rushed into the kitchen to see what had happened. They found glass all over the stove.

"My stew," Martha shouted. "It's ruined. I don't understand what happened."

"I changed the light bulb as you asked me to; that should not have happened. "stammered George.

"What kind of light bulb did you use?" she questioned.

"Just a regular 100-watt bulb. Oops, I should have used the light bulb that is made for stoves. No wonder it blew. When the steam hit the light bulb, that's why it popped. Sorry, I wasn't thinking. I'll clean up this mess. I hope we have something else for dinner.

"Good excuse for a pizza dinner, I'll call," replied Martha. "They'll be here by the time we clean up this mess. Too bad, that was a perfectly good stew."

They were a bit shaken, not stirred.' 4Dinner was a success before retiring for the night.

The Future

The future is a space in time that has not happened. Yet, people try to guess, wish, and pray that it will favor them. Prophets have been predicting the future for centuries. I am sure even the cavemen wondered, what would tomorrow bring? What fish would they catch, or what animal would they kill for dinner? They might have wondered if it would rain or if a storm was on the horizon. All these things are questions of the future.

What teenager hasn't worried about who will be their date? Who will be their friend after High School? Who will they marry, and how many children will they have? What will they have to look forward to? How many children will they have? What occupation will they choose? Everything is in the future. Of course, those questions are all answered in time.

When we get old, we wonder, how long do I have? What will my health be like? Will I be able to live on my own? Where will the money come from? All questions of future events of everyday living. It is human nature to wonder and plan for things to come,

There are ancient prophecies, world prophecies, and prophecies in every culture back to the beginning of time.

There are some that chart the stars by the way they move in the night sky. They seek to predict what will become of us. Their equipment was simple. High-powered telescopes were not available as they are today. Hundreds of years ago, the sky was much different than the sky we see today. Stars change, and so does how we see the stars. It has also been rumored that a great meteor will hit the Earth. Will we be able to reflect it? I think they're still working on that.

There are some that have visions of what is to come. They see pictures in their mind. Their visions are not always understood. They are often misinterpreted. The psychics who help solve murder cases see numbers, objects, and places. Putting all the clues together to mean something is difficult, even for the person seeing the vision.

Whatever the technique, it was charged by an anxiety to know what lies ahead for themselves or for others. However, visions come without warning. I have read many prophecies. I became interested in a man named Michel de Nostradamus, born on December 14, 1503. His knowledge and the way he thought was not excepted in those days. He was a visionary of his time. He wrote what is called "Quatrains." His look into the future. In several of these "Quatrains," he mentions a place called the New City. It is common knowledge that the name refers to New York City. I read a Quatrain that I knew was an interest to many people, especially in the East. If you live in New York City or the surrounding states, it will raise more attention than it would on the west coast. I read one of these Quatrains and knew exactly what it meant. I told several people who were also curious about the meaning. I also told a person of authority. I told myself to say nothing while others laughed and disregarded it completely.

One prominent friend was very upset that I would think to reveal a different conclusion than already stated by authors who have written books on the life and times of Nostradamus. I was warned to say nothing because my interpretation would give those who would harm us ideas. I was devastated but agreed to say nothing. I didn't want anything to happen because of what I knew. This was 20 years ago. Putting this idea out of my mind was seriously affecting my everyday living. Having read so many other prophecies took its toll on me. I was afraid to face another day, terrified another day wouldn't exist. I tried to keep busy with new activities but to no avail. After about 2 years passed, I convinced myself to live for the present. If tomorrow isn't there, then so be it. I slowly accepted the idea; I was to say nothing.

Recently a fellow writer wrote about the end of the world. What would happen to us and to our children? I immediately recoiled and fled. I did not want to think of all those prophecies I managed to put behind me. It was too late. All the prophecies came to mind once more, taunting me, pulling me back to where I was 20 years earlier.

Sleep was not forthcoming. I awoke every few hours. My appetite was slight. I felt stressed without a way to get past this. I wandered around the house, rearranging furniture. (My favorite thing to do when I'm upset).

There was only one answer. I would have to write about the one thing I was warned not to. The interpretation had to be told.

Many writers have associated quatrain 49 with the disastrous day of 911. I don't think that was it. All the pieces do not fit. That catastrophe was truly a blow to thousands and affected the lives of all of us.

Security was tightened in all airports. Background checks were questioned more closely. People became scared of what was to come next. Especially the people in the East near New York. I'm sure when Mt. St. Helena blew, the west coast was devastated. It took weeks to clear the roads and dust off cars and all their belongings, not to mention the lives that were lost. The effect was not as severe in the East. They felt sympathy for those but could not possibly know how it felt. In order to properly interpret Quatrain 49, it is necessary to know the east coast and where things are. You couldn't find an address unless you knew the street and which town it was in. The Quatrain was translated to read:

Garden of the new world near the new city,

In the path of the hollow mountains: It will be seized and plunged into the Tub,

Forced to drink waters poisoned by sulfur.

"Garden of the new world," I believe, refers to New Jersey. New Jersey is called

"The Garden State" because Abraham Browning of Camden, In his address, compared New Jersey to an immense barrel filled with good things to eat and open at both ends, Pennsylvanians grabbing from one end and New Yorkers from the other. He called New Jersey the "Garden State", and the name has clung to it ever since.

Next, it says, "Near the new city." It doesn't say it takes place in New York. It says, (keyword), NEAR the new city. So that means it's not New York at all, only near it.

"In the path of the hollow mountains." I have read many versions of this sentence. Some say that they think it refers to the Holland Tunnel in New York and/or the subway systems below ground. However, it does

137

say near, not in the city. I believe the hollow mountains mentioned in the next line are beyond New York and New Jersey. They are the mountains of Pennsylvania.

When I was very young, I remember visiting someone in Pennsylvania. I don't remember who, but I remember those tunnels that go through the mountains. There were so many of them. Tunnel after tunnel after tunnel. I didn't think I was going to make it out alive. The exhaust fumes that built up inside the tunnels were unbearable. I tried to cover my nose each time we went through a tunnel. After every tunnel we would roll down the windows to get some fresh air. I was elated to reach our destination. The highway I am referring to is. The nepheline is, "It will be seized and plunged into the tub." This, too, is clear as crystal. At the end of that highway is a nuclear plant. Our enemy will seize the plant and destroy the facility. The Tub refers to the nuclear tower. The tower is fueled by a yellow liquid which is radioactive. Liquid fluoride thorium reactor, the fission of U-233 in the core heats molten carrier salt (yellow).

"forced to drink water poisoned by sulfur" is obviously radioactive fluid from the plant, poisoning a great deal of land. I believe Nostradamus did not recognize the fluid as radioactive but could only describe it as sulfur, which is the only substance he knew. Sulfur is yellow in color. I know that if this does happen, it will be an even bigger catastrophe than 911. The land will be contaminated for years. Many people will lose everything they own and even their lives. It will become another "Chernobyl." Plus, power will be lost for thousands of people.

Can this happen in the US.? We hope not. However, forewarned is forearmed.

Although many new safety features have been installed and the "tub" is extremely thick concrete, it can still be sabotaged and destroyed.

The reason I decided to write this version of the interpreted Quatrain is to warn those powers that be. If they will take this seriously, then maybe we can prevent another disaster; knowledge in advance is an invaluable tool. Had the Titanic been forewarned, it would still be sailing today. If we were forewarned, 911 would not have happened.

Even the strongest threshold can be destroyed from the inside out. The enemy does not always strike from the outside in. Case in point — The Trojan Horse.

The End

The Unicorn

While strolling through some small shops in Spokane, the young Alice
Found a little store on a little side street. The shop was old and tattered.
An antique sign hung over the door. In the window was a statue of a fine
porcelain unicorn. It was a multi-colored white with a tint of pink swirling
through the finely delicate lines.

Alice's eyes widened as she continued her gaze. Never had she seen
such a beautiful unicorn. With a song in her heart, she entered the little
shop. Ornate candlesticks and dusty furniture filled the store. Old lamps
and many nick-nacks caught her eye.

"Hello, is anyone here?" she called out.

A little old woman appeared from behind a curtain. "I am here," she
answered in a squeaky voice.

"I was interested in the unicorn in the window; it is very beautiful."

"I'm afraid it's not for sale. It is my favorite piece. Can I interest you
in something else?" she questioned.

"No, I really love the unicorn. Please, I really would love to buy it."
Alice pleaded.

"I'm sorry, dear, it's really not for sale, replied the old woman. Alice
started to walk toward the door. Her heart felt heavy as she bowed her
head. She stopped to admire the unicorn once more,

The old woman suddenly grabbed her arm. "excuse me miss, you
seem to really like that piece. Well, I'm old, and I really want it to have a
good home. I can't sell it to you, but I will give it to you if you promise to
take good care of it, and I think you will."

"Yes, oh yes, I have never seen a unicorn so elegantly beautiful."
"Wait one moment, and I will wrap it up for you. I brave a nice box I can
put it in; I've saved it for such an occasion. The old woman disappeared

and returned with the box and carefully placed it inside. She put the box in a small shopping bag and handed it to Alice.

"Thank you so much," Alice exclaimed. She hugged the old woman and left the store smiling and happy.

Alice, arriving home sometime later, placed the unicorn on her mantle over the fireplace. She sat and stared at it for a long time. Sleep filled her head as she drifted off to dreamland.

The next day Alice decided to take some lunch to the old woman. It was the least she could do. She packed a nice lunch and went straight to the store. "Hello, is anyone here," she cried, "I thought I'd bring you some lunch. It's the least I can do," called Alice.

A young man entered the room, "Can I help you?"

"I was looking for the older woman I talked to yesterday. She gave me a unicorn of very fine quality."

"That couldn't have been yesterday. The store was closed. I had to go to an Estate Sale to pick up some items. What did she look like?

As Alice described her, the young man's eyes widened, "That's my grandmother; she left me this store ten years ago. She always had a favorite unicorn. How she loved it."

Alice gasped, "She gave me a unicorn yesterday."

As they talked, They both realized what a bazaar situation brought them together.

"So, I'm Earl; what is your name."

"My name is Alice, Alice Walker," she said shyly

"So, Alice can I take you to dinner, he smiled.

"Only if you will have lunch with me now."

They smiled at each other and enjoyed a most wonderful lunch, one of many more to come.

The Long Trip Home

In the fall of 1953, my Dad persuaded my Mom to move from Nova Scotia, Canada, to the United States because my Dad was in the Merchant Marines and could only come home on an average of once a year. They sold the house and everything in it. My two brothers and I were very perplexed, but the choice had been made.

Dad made all the arrangements, and in what seemed like a very short time, we found ourselves at the border between the United States and Canada. I felt something was wrong when they took us inside, and we had to sit while Mom and Dad were taken to the office. A short time later, they emerged. "Sorry, kids, but we have to go back," declared my Mom. "We can't go back; there's no place for us to sleep," we protested. Mom assured us we could stay with my Grandmother we called Nanna. "I don't have the proper papers. It will only be for a few days," she said, trying to comfort us. There were hugs all around as we made our way back to Nanna's house.

Once there, we were greeted with a banquet and a house full of family members. The smell of baked beans and apple pie filled the air.

Three days later, we were told all the paperwork was cleared, and we could leave again. This time we were going on a ship. To get there, we had to take the train.

I remember standing on the platform when that monstrous machine pulled up in front of me. I think I must have screamed because everyone came running toward us, especially the conductor. He helped us up on the train. It seemed higher than a house.

Once inside, it didn't seem so scary, and I curled up on the seat and fell asleep next to my two brothers. It was a short trip, and soon we were unloading again.

We made our way down to the dock to catch the next ship sailing for the US. My Dad herded us into a big lounge. We sat on the side, wondering what to do next. It was night, and we should be in bed. Dad left momentarily and returned in a hurry. "We're in for it," he declared. "I was just up at the bar, and they are covering them with wet towels." "what does that mean," asked my Mom. "It means a storm is coming, and it's going to get rough."

My Dad reached into his pocket and gave us all a little pill. "This will help," he said calmly.

Late that night, I had to go to the bathroom. I woke my Mom, and she took me by the hand to the Lady's Room. We were horrified to see such a sight. Everyone must have had Spaghetti for dinner. There was sauce and noodles everywhere. My Mom took me over to the sink. Cleaned off a corner and promptly sat me up there. Everyone was so sick no one seemed to care. It was difficult as the ship swayed. When we got back to the lounge, everyone was wide awake. Dad offered to give everyone a tour of the ship, but I was the only one willing. He took me up and down and everywhere. It was a most special time with my Dad. As we made our way back to the lounge, we saw a sailor coming down the stairs. The ship pitched, and he went flying forward. My Dad laughed so hard. "He couldn't have been at sea very long; everyone knows you walk down backward to have a better grip." he laughed again.

We made it through the storm and were once again on our way. My Dad's brother was there to pick us up. We all loaded in the car, and it was out like a light. We arrived in Bridgeport, Connecticut, sometime in the afternoon. Our uncle had secured an apartment in the city. So many buildings so close together. The Apartment was so small it didn't even have a bathtub. It did have an indoor toilet, and I had my own room. We all slept 'til the next day. So, this was home. I didn't question it, I just accepted it, but it sure was a long way home.

Orange

I've orange this skit for Aunt Sid
Orange, you glad that I did,
I rhymed a thing or two
from dressing up with Peggy Sue
The dress she wore was orange
The color was dull and borage
Orange is not for me
unless the color is cree
The rhyme just doesn't matter
like orange juice, it likes to splatter
I'd rather have pink, maybe blue
instead of orange, don't you?
ranging things in order
was a gift from Mother Hoarder
with lemons and limes in her drawer
No oranges could be found
Cause she fed them all to her hound,

Printed in the United States
by Baker & Taylor Publisher Services

Printed in the United States
by Baker & Taylor Publisher Services